This book belongs to

....

CONTENTS

Rupert and the Iceberg 6
From The Rupert Annual *1986. Illustrated by* John Harrold.

Rupert and the Fiddle 21
From The Rupert Annual *1968. Illustrated by* Alfred Bestall.

Rupert and the Green Man 45
Story originated and illustrated by Stuart Trotter.
Text and couplets written by Mara Alperin.

Spot the Difference 60

Rupert and the Gardens Mystery 61
From The Rupert Annual *1992. Illustrated by* John Harrold.

How Rupert Makes a Paper Lily 78
From The Rupert Annual *1968.*

Rupert and the Gemlins 80
From The Rupert Annual *1982. Illustrated by* Jennifer Kisler.

Rupert and the Snowball 98
From The Rupert Annual *1969. Illustrated by* Alfred Bestall.

Edited by Mara Alperin. *Designed by* Pritty Ramjee.
Cover illustrated by Stuart Trotter.
Endpapers illustrated by Alfred Bestall.

THE RUPERT® ANNUAL

EXPRESS NEWSPAPERS

EGMONT
We bring stories to life

Published in Great Britain 2016 by Egmont UK Limited
The Yellow Building, 1 Nicholas Road, London W11 4AN
Rupert Bear™ & © Express Newspapers & DreamWorks Distribution Limited.
All Rights Reserved.

ISBN 978 1 4052 8351 9
63784/1
Printed in Italy

All rights reserved. No part of this publication may be reproduced, stored in a retrieval system or transmitted, in any form or by
any means, mechanical, photocopying, recording or otherwise, without the prior permission of the publisher and copyright holder.
Stay safe online. Any website addresses listed in this book are correct at the time of going to print. However, Egmont is not
responsible for content hosted by third parties. Please be aware that online content can be subject to change and websites can
contain content that is unsuitable for children. We advise that all children are supervised when using the internet.

No. 81

RUPERT
CLASSIC™

RUPERT and

"It's really hot. I think I'll take
A dip since I'm so near the lake."

Phew! It *is* hot! And Rupert is beginning to feel that this isn't really the sort of weather for a ramble on the common. Then he spots the lake below and suddenly a dip in it seems very attractive. So down he goes and he has just got there when he hears a splash. Someone else with the same idea, he thinks. But, no! The splash is followed by a cry for help. Rupert dashes towards the sound of more splashing.

1075236/JF

the ICEBERG

A cry! A splash! An awful din!
"My goodness! Someone's fallen in!"

"I'm coming!" Rupert gives a shout,
And finds an old man climbing out.

On a stretch of bank shaded by a big tree he finds an old man with a long beard trying to climb out of the water. With Rupert's help the old man scrambles ashore. "Are you all right?" Rupert asks anxiously. "Yes, apart from being soaked," the man replies. "I foolishly leant over too far with my net . . . and, ah, yes, there it is. Would you be a good little bear and get it ashore for me? I should hate to lose it."

Although the old man's sopping wet,
He's more concerned about his net.

RUPERT IS PUZZLED BY WEEDS

"Oh, please," the old man begs, "be quick!"
So Rupert gets it with a stick.

"I'll throw the weeds out," Rupert cries.
"No! Don't do that!" the man replies.

"Now, come along and you shall see
Why those weeds mean so much to me."

And in his house the old man shows
Tanks full of water plants in rows.

Wondering why the old man is so concerned about a fishing net when he is standing there soaked to the skin, Rupert gets a stick and manages to pull the net to the bank. The old man is delighted and Rupert is very curious to see what the net holds that can affect him like this. But it has only water-weeds in it. "I'll tip these back," he says. "No, no!" cries the old man. "I want them. Those weeds are what I was fishing for when I fell in."

Then the old man sees the look on Rupert's face and chuckles: "I can see you don't understand. Well, if you care to follow me to my house . . ." He points to a mansion on the far shore. "I shall explain." And off he scampers at a surprising rate with Rupert at his heels. In the mansion he leads the way to a room lined with glass tanks. "Stay here and have a look," he invites Rupert. "I'm going off to change." The tanks, Rupert sees, are full of water plants.

RUPERT GETS AN INVITATION

"I'm flying to the far North where
A seaweed grows that's very rare."

"And, if you like, you may come, too.
Go home and ask. I'll wait for you."

Though it's still very hot next day,
With coat and scarf he's on his way.

"So glad you're coming, little bear.
We're going in my seaplane there."

"Now," the old man says when he returns, "you see why I didn't want those weeds thrown back. I am a collector of water plants and I have almost every kind." It seems an odd thing to collect but Rupert politely looks interested and the old man goes on about his hobby over tea and later as he walks back part of the way with Rupert. "I'm going north tomorrow to look for a very rare plant," he says. "You may care to come too?" "Ooh, yes!" says Rupert.

So Rupert and the old man agree to meet next day near what looks like a huge boat-house. "And bring warm clothes," the old man says. "It must be very far north if you need warm clothes at this time of year," says Mrs Bear. But she agrees to his going, and off he sets next day carrying coat and scarf. When he gets to where they are to meet he finds the old man in flying gear and, out on the lake, a big seaplane. "We are taking my aircraft," the old man says.

RUPERT FLIES NORTH

They climb aboard. The engines roar.
Then off towards the North they soar.

High over northern seas they go,
And there's the place they want, below.

The man says, "This takes time, I've found.
So why don't you just look around?"

He wonders, looking out to sea,
"Whatever can those white rocks be?"

"So this is what was in that huge boat-shed," Rupert thinks as he climbs aboard the seaplane. The old man must be very well-off to be able to afford such a machine. Then the engines burst into life, the seaplane skims over the lake and a minute later they are high over Nutwood, heading north. Soon the summery countryside is far behind and they are over a cold-looking sea. By the time they reach where they're going Rupert is glad he brought his coat and scarf.

It is a bleak, rocky place where the pair come ashore. "Now, this weed-hunting can take a bit of time," the old man says. "So, why don't you do a bit of scrambling about and exploring to keep yourself warm?" That seems a good idea and off goes Rupert, promising to be careful. He likes climbing and makes his way to the top of a little headland. And there, out to sea, he sees something he has never seen before. "What lovely white rocks those are!" he marvels.

RUPERT MEETS SAILOR SAM

Then Rupert hears a cheery shout,
And from a hut a tar comes out.

"Rocks, you say?" he laughs. "That's droll!
They're icebergs! See, we're near the Pole."

"Then Uncle Polar must live near.
Look, that's him in this snapshot here."

The sailor – name of Sam – says, "We
Can take the boat I've here with me."

Suddenly Rupert finds himself being hailed from somewhere below. He climbs down a little way, and there is a motorboat, a hut and an old-fashioned sailor – the sort who used to be called Jack Tar. This one, though, turns out to be called Sailor Sam who has been fishing. Well, of course, the first thing Rupert asks about is the "white rocks". "Rocks?" cries Sam. "They're not rocks! They're icebergs! We're not so far from the North Pole here." The North Polc!

The words have Rupert searching his pockets. Yes, here it is! He produces a snapshot and shows it to Sam. "My Uncle Polar Bear!" he says. "He sent me this picture at Christmas. He lives near the Pole." "Then why don't we visit him?" laughs Sam. "My boat's a fast little craft. We could be there and back in no time!" "Oh, could we?" Rupert cries. "I'd love to!" And so, with Sam's promise to get him back in good time, Rupert scrambles down to the boat.

RUPERT GOES FURTHER NORTH

"It shouldn't be too long a run,"
Says Sam. And Rupert thinks, "What fun!"

Now more and more icebergs appear
As even further north they steer.

Says Sam, "Now off you go and find
Your uncle. I shall stay behind."

"Oh, please," he asks, "do you know where
I may find Mr Polar Bear?"

Sam holds the boat steady while Rupert climbs into it. "It's not much to look at," he says. "But it's sturdy and nippy, as you'll see." Sure enough, the little boat cuts through the water at a cracking pace. "This is fun!" Rupert laughs, and Sam agrees, for it's pretty boring just fishing by yourself day after day and the trip makes a pleasant break. As they near their destination the icebergs get more and more numerous. "I should hate to hit one," says Rupert. At last Sam stops and moors on an ice-bound shore. "Now, off you go and find your uncle," he tells Rupert. "Take this compass to help you find your way back. I'll stay here and fish." Of course, Rupert doesn't know exactly where his uncle lives but guesses that the local creatures will, and so he stops and asks some puffins, "Please, can you tell me where Mr Polar Bear lives?" A sea-swallow who overhears this pipes up, "Yes, I know where. Come on, I'll show you."

RUPERT VISITS HIS UNCLE

A friendly sea-bird leads him to
His Uncle Polar Bear's igloo.

There's not a sign of life to see,
But on he trudges cheerfully.

When he arrives he gives a shout
And Uncle Polar Bear pops out.

His uncle can't believe his eyes.
"But how did you get here?" he cries.

They don't have to go far before the sea-swallow stops and says, "There!" Rupert looks over the barren white landscape. "Where?" he asks. "There!" says the bird and indicates what looks like a mound of snow. So Rupert thanks the bird and sets off for the mound. There's not a sign of life to be seen but Rupert trudges on cheerfully and as he gets close, he thinks, "Of course, it's an igloo sort of thing. I suppose I was expecting a house something like ours."

Unlike the usual sort of igloo this one doesn't have any sort of entrance. So Rupert has to stand outside and shout, "Uncle!" He jumps when a hole is punched in the snow wall and a large head appears. "Good gracious!" it says. Then more snow is kicked out to make a doorway of sorts and out steps Uncle Polar Bear. "Rupert!" he cries. "What a lovely surprise. Now come inside at once and tell me how on earth you come to be here." Inside there is only a bed and a stove.

*"Our winter lasts for half a year.
You could be trapped that long up here."*

*"If that is so, I mustn't stay.
I only came out for the day."*

*"Then off you go now!" Uncle cries
"Or night will catch you by surprise."*

*So Rupert, waving, turns to go.
His tracks are still plain in the snow.*

Uncle Polar rustles up a hot drink for Rupert and then he says something strange: "I suppose you have brought your bed." "Bed?" repeats Rupert. "But why should I?" And then he learns something which alarms him. "Well, winter lasts for months up here," his uncle says. "It's dark all the time so we sleep right through it . . . and it's almost on us now." He points to the disappearing sun. "Oh, dear, I'm only here for the day!" Rupert cries. "I must be off at once!"

Of course, Uncle Polar is sorry Rupert can't stay longer. But he quite understands. "Now, hurry," he says, "or you may be caught by the long winter night. You must visit me again some other time – but not at this time of year." So Rupert says goodbye to Uncle Polar, promises to give his best wishes to Mr and Mrs Bear, and sets off back to Sam and the boat. "It shouldn't take long," he tells himself. "All I need do is follow the tracks I made coming here."

RUPERT LOSES THE COMPASS

But now as snow begins to fall,
He cannot see his tracks at all.

He shouts, and to his great delight,
He hears Sam calling, "You're all right!"

But Rupert's lost – and this is grim –
The compass that Sam lent to him.

By now the snowstorm's so severe
That Sam decides they can't stay here.

But it is not to be as easy as that. Rupert has not been going long when a strong wind rises and it begins to snow. In no time his tracks vanish. This is frightening. Nothing but a whirling whiteness all around him. Gamely he plods on, but he has no way of knowing if he is going the right way. How awful it would be to get lost out here with the long winter night coming on! The thought so frightens him that he shouts, "Sam! Help!"

And a great wave of relief sweeps over him when Sam's voice calls back, "You're all right!" When Sam hears what Uncle Polar has said about the winter night starting he says, "Then we best be off now. Just let me have the compass I lent you." Rupert reaches into his pocket. No compass! "I've lost it!" he wails. "Then we must take our chances," Sam declares. "Anything's better than being trapped here all winter." So the two scramble into the boat and head into the storm.

RUPERT IS WRECKED

They battle on through raging seas.
As darkness falls the two friends freeze.

A sudden crash! And Rupert squeals
As both are flung head over heels.

They aren't hurt, but nonetheless,
Poor Sam's boat is an awful mess!

When the storm dies they see the boat,
As it is now, could never float.

The storm rises, the seas get rougher and the wind drives the snow ever more fiercely against Rupert and Sam. As near as he can tell, Sam holds his course, and though it gets darker and darker he does not slacken speed. It is too important to get well away from the land of the long night. Rupert is thinking how lucky it is that the boat is such a sturdy one when – *Crrrash!* The front of the boat seems to explode and the two friends are pitched head over heels!

What Rupert feared earlier has happened. They have struck an iceberg. Luckily neither is hurt and they huddle into what shelter they can find, waiting for the storm to blow itself out. When at last it passes, and its darkness with it, Rupert and Sam survey the damage. It's terrible. Only the back part of the little craft has survived. The front half is smashed beyond repair – fit only for firewood. It is plain that the brave little boat's days are over.

RUPERT HAS A BRAINWAVE

Now Sam slumps down in deep despair.
But Rupert says, "The rudder's there."

So to the ice the boat they rope.
And now at least they have a hope.

"The engine works!" Sam shouts with glee.
"The iceberg's now our boat, you see!"

It's clumsy and it's very slow.
But, still, towards the South they go.

It's all too much for Sam and he slumps down in despair. Then Rupert who has been examining what's left of the boat says, "Sam, the rudder and the propeller are perfectly all right . . . I've got an idea if they can be made to work. Do we have any rope?" "Yes," says Sam, "But what . . . ?" "Then help me to get the stern back into the water and we'll lash the boat to the iceberg." Sam's face lights up as he gets the idea. And in no time the pair are working busily.

At last they are ready. Will the engine work? They hold their breath as Sam works the starter. Oh, great! The engine bursts into life. Now the whole iceberg is their boat. A slow, clumsy boat. But it is moving, that's what is important. And with Sam holding the rudder lines and steering by sun and stars, it is moving in the right direction, away from the dangerous Polar seas and the long, long night. Rupert sits on the peak of the iceberg acting as lookout.

RUPERT IS REALLY WORRIED

Just as they think the worst is past
They find the iceberg's melting fast.

And then the engine loses speed!
Somehow it's got all choked with weed.

Sam says, "We're done for now, I fear.
The ice won't last much longer here."

Despairingly he tries again . . .
But look! Yes, it's the old man's plane!

As the strange iceberg-craft moves slowly south the two friends notice something they might have expected. As the air gets warmer the iceberg is melting. Can they reach land before it melts away altogether? There's nothing for it but to keep going. Then when the iceberg is no more than a quarter of its old size, the engine stops and Sam can't re-start it. When he scrambles to the stern and looks he sees why. The propeller is entangled in thick seaweed.

Desperately he tries to clear the weed. But after what seems ages he has managed to free only a few strands. "Oh, Sam, the iceberg will melt in half an hour!" Rupert groans. "Then I think we are done for," says Sam. "I can't move the rest of the stuff in that time." But he keeps trying, though with almost no success. Suddenly Rupert's sharp ears pick up a droning. He gazes skywards. He can hardly believe his eyes. "Sam!" he yells. "It's the old man's seaplane!"

RUPERT IS RESCUED

The old man spots the boat, descends
And taxies over to the friends.

1075236/JF

And as he throws the pair a rope,
He says, "I almost gave up hope."

To what Sam says he pays no heed.
His eyes are fastened on the weed.

"Oh, my!" he gasps. "This weed you caught
Is just the very thing I sought!"

The old man has spotted Rupert's wildly waving scarf and eases the big seaplane down on to the water. Gently he taxies over to the iceberg-craft so as not to swamp it. He climbs from the cockpit with a length of rope, which he ties to one of the float struts before throwing the other end to Sam. Then when the seaplane is close enough he jumps on to the rapidly melting iceberg. "What on earth happened to you?" he asks Rupert. "I'd almost given up hope of seeing you again!"

Sam starts to tell about how he took Rupert to see his uncle and agrees that they ought to have told the old man first . . . Then he stops. For the old man isn't listening to him. His eyes are fastened on the seaweed that Sam is still clutching. He takes it from Sam's hand and gazes at it. The other two look at each other and wonder what's happening. Then the old man speaks: "This is amazing! The very seaweed I flew north to find. I found none. But you have!"

RUPERT GOES HOME

"Now, Sam," he says, "I'll bear the cost
Of making good the boat you've lost."

As they take off and start to climb.
The wreck sinks. They were just in time!

It's so nice to be home again,
With Daddy there to meet the plane.

And finally the old man gives
Our Sam the shack where he still lives!

The old man could not be more delighted. "Oh, well," says Sam, "thank goodness someone has got something out of this sorry business." And he gazes at the remains of his boat. "My dear sir," cries the old man. "You must not suffer by this adventure which has ended so well for me. I shall pay for a new boat for you!" Then he looks about him at the dwindling iceberg. "But I think we should be going right now." So they climb into the seaplane and go – not a moment too soon!

Mr Bear is waiting anxiously when Rupert and the others return. "My goodness, you had us worried," he says. "Me too," laughs the old man. Now everything is fine . . . except that Sailor Sam, it turns out, has no home to go to. "Then I have just the place for you!" cries the old man. And he leads the way to a roomy, well-built shack on his estate. Sam is speechless with delight. So is Rupert who has come to like Sam. And to this day he often has tea at Sam's place.

RUPERT
and the
FIDDLE

It is meant to make sweet music for a royal person, but when Simple Simon tries to play a tune the noise is simply dreadful! Rupert doesn't like it. Neither does the merry old soul whom he meets during his adventure.

RUPERT STOPS TO LISTEN

"What was that noise?" says Rupert Bear.
"It seemed to come from over there."

The others think it's just a game.
"There are no noises!" they exclaim.

"All right!" calls Rupert. "Just you wait!
I'm going to investigate!"

He wanders on, until he sees
A figure moving through the trees.

Rupert is out with his best pals Bill Badger and Algy Pug, and they are just wondering what game to play when the little bear comes to a stop. For some minutes he gazes round in a puzzled way. At last Bill breaks the silence. "What's up with him?" he asks. "Hi, Rupert, have you seen something?" "N-no, but I've heard something," says Rupert. "At least I think I have. Listen. Can you hear it too?" The others keep very quiet but can't hear a thing.

"There isn't any noise," laughs Algy. "Rupert's having us on!" Rupert insists that he has heard a mysterious sound, though the others, in spite of trying very hard, can still hear nothing. "I wish I knew where it was coming from," murmurs the little bear. "I *think* it's in this direction." Rupert keeps on until he is well out of sight. All at once he pauses and peeps over a bush. On the opposite side a strange figure in gaudy clothes has appeared between the trees from the wood.

RUPERT STARTLES THE MAN

The stranger pauses in surprise.
"Alas! I have been seen!" he sighs.

"I've slipped away from work, you see!
I want to take the whole day free!"

"That wood's the safest place for you.
The windmill is deserted, too."

"To think he gets no holidays!
What can his work be?" Rupert says.

The colourful stranger does not see Rupert until he is nearly upon him and then he gives a startled gasp. "Nay, but 'tis a little bear!" he exclaims. "Alas, I had not meant to be seen by anybody." "But please, people can't help seeing you in those lovely clothes," says Rupert in surprise. "Are you trying to hide from somebody?" "Not exactly that," replies the man. "I am on a day's holiday, my first for many years. If the king, my master, knew he would be very angry, for I have taken it without permission." Rupert looks at the friendly stranger. "Well, if you don't want to be seen by anyone you'll need to walk in our quietest parts, won't you? Why not go down there? There will be nobody in those other woods and the windmill is deserted just now." "In sooth that would please me greatly," says the man. He hurries off and Rupert climbs part way up a tree to watch him. "I wish I had the courage to ask who he is," mutters the little bear. "He looks jolly interesting."

RUPERT IS NOT PRETENDING

"Hi Algy! Bill! You'll never guess!
I met a man in olden dress!"

But Algy shakes with merriment,
"What fairy tales you do invent!"

Then Rupert hears that noise once more,
And tries to trace it, as before.

"Hello there, Reggie! Have you heard
A high, thin sound? It's not a bird."

When the stranger has gone Rupert realises that he has not heard the tiny mysterious noise for some time so he turns to rejoin his pals. "Well, did you trace that sound that we couldn't hear?" demands Bill. "No," Rupert admits, "but I saw something odder still, a man in a flat cap, striped tunic, long stockings and . . ." "There, what did I tell you!" cries Algy, laughing. "Rupert was teasing us about that noise and now he has made up an even better fairy tale for us!" Rupert doesn't mind being laughed at by his pals. "I'm not teasing you about that noise," he smiles. "I believe you're teasing me by pretending that you can't hear it!" Just then he is sure that he can hear the noise again and he moves off in an effort to get nearer to it. In some bushes Reggie Rabbit is looking for early blackberries. "Hello, Reggie," Rupert calls. "You're just the person I want. Tell me, have you been hearing a high, thin sound? Bill and Algy think I have been imagining it."

RUPERT MEANS TO FIND OUT

"Why, no!" says Reggie, with a frown,
And then the others scamper down.

"You're only teasing, we can tell!
Or we should hear that sound as well!"

"The noise is like a squeal or wheeze.
It's not the buzzing of those bees!"

The three watch Rupert turn away.
"I'll prove I'm right," they hear him say.

In some surprise Reggie listens carefully. "N-no, I can't hear anything at all," he says. As he listens again the other pals come scampering to join them. "Well, have you found someone else to play your tricks on," laughs Algy. "What a chap you are, Rupert, to keep up your fairy tale so long! How do you manage to keep so serious about it?" "It's not a fairy tale, honestly it isn't," Rupert declares. "There really is a tiny noise and it's very odd if Reggie with his big, long ears can't hear it too." Rupert begins to get worried about the mysterious noise. "If only I knew which direction it was coming from I could go towards it," he mutters. "It's so tiny that I can't tell if it's near or far away. If it is near it might be those bees: but no, it isn't a buzzing sound. I just don't know how to describe it." His pals watch him as he moves away slowly. "I will find what it is," says Rupert, his curiosity now thoroughly aroused. "I'll prove that I'm not making it up."

RUPERT WANDERS ON ALONE

"Let's take no notice, then it's plain
He'll just have to come back again!"

A stoat looks up, as Rupert speaks.
"Of course I've heard that noise!" it squeaks.

"It's simply awful, no mistake!
It makes my poor head ache and ache!"

"Ooh-oh! It's right behind me now!"
Gasps Rupert. "What a dreadful row!"

Rupert's pals watch him walking slowly away as if he has forgotten them. "He's playing his game jolly well," Bill laughs. "It must be a game, since none of us can hear the noise he speaks of. Let's just wait and pretend to forget him. He's sure to come back." However, Rupert carries on, listening all the time, and sometimes catching the sound quite clearly. "Whatever is it? I've never heard it before," he murmurs. Near a hedge he comes across a large stoat. "Wait a minute, don't run and hide," he says. "I've a question to ask that you may be able to answer. I've been hearing a strange wailing noise. My pals think I'm playing a game with them, but I'm not. Have you heard it?" "Heard it!" squeaks the stoat, scowling savagely. "I should think I have. It keeps on, and it's horrible. It's coming from over there." Delighted to be given the right direction, Rupert runs on. For a moment the sound ceases. Then as he passes a wood it suddenly starts again.

RUPERT DISCOVERS SIMON

A lad peeps round the leafy clump,
And chuckles, "Did I make you jump?"

"I found this in a hollow tree!"
Cries Simple Simon. "Come and see!"

"A fiddle!" gasps the little bear,
"Whoever can have left it there?"

"Oh, my! He cannot play a note!
No wonder he upset that stoat!"

Feeling very excited at being so near to the mysterious noise, Rupert pushes into the wood. Almost at once he comes face to face with a cheerful young figure. "Why, if it isn't Simple Simon," he exclaims. "Whatever are you doing here? Were you making that awful noise? Surely that wasn't you trying to sing!" "Don't be silly," laughs Simon. "Did it sound like singing? Come, and I'll show you what I've found." He leads the way to a hollow tree and from it takes a curious old fiddle and bow. Rupert takes the strange fiddle and looks at it curiously. "I've never seen one like this before," he says. "Whose is it? And why was it left in such a place as that? And did the noise that has been puzzling me come from this?" "I've been playing it," says Simon. "It's not difficult. I'll do it again." He takes the bow and begins to play. "Oh my!" thinks Rupert. "It sounded queer from a long way off, but this is terrible! No wonder that stoat was so upset."

RUPERT WALKS A LONG WAY

"You can't just leave it there again!
Supposing it comes on to rain!"

The lad agrees, and so they plan
To find the owner, if they can.

But though they keep a sharp look-out,
There isn't anyone about.

"Oh dear! We've wandered much too far,
And now I don't know where we are!"

To Rupert's relief the boy soon stops playing. "There, I've had some good practice with that," says Simple Simon. "I'm a jolly good player, aren't I?" Rupert doesn't like to answer that and he watches the other put the fiddle back into the hollow tree. "Hi, we mustn't leave it there in case it gets wet," he calls. "We'd better take it with us if we're going to find the owner or to give it to Constable Growler." Simon returns and hangs the fiddle over his shoulder by its strap.

The two friends wander away, Simon carrying the strange fiddle and Rupert holding the bow, and keeping a sharp look-out for anyone who looks as if he might be the owner. They try to walk in a circle, but there are lots of slopes and little hills and after a while Rupert stops and gazes round. "I say, I don't know these parts," he calls uneasily. "Have you any idea where we are?" "N-no," says Simple Simon nervously. "I thought you were leading and knew the way. Oh dear!"

RUPERT SPIES TWO RIDERS

"Perhaps if someone hears me play,
They'll come, then we could ask the way."

"That would drive them off instead,"
Sighs Rupert. "How it hurts my head!"

Then, as the chums are losing hope,
Two horsemen canter down the slope.

The little bear runs very fast,
And stops the men from riding past.

"If only that deserted windmill was in sight I should know where to go," says Rupert. "As it is I'm quite lost." "Well, cheer up," says Simple Simon. "I've just had a notion. You came to me when I was playing. If I could play again it might attract someone else. Then we can ask them the way home." Rupert sits down while the boy scrapes happily on the fiddle. "Oh dear," mutters the little bear. "I don't think that would attract anybody. It would drive them away!"

Rupert endures the noise as long as he can, then suggests that they walk on. They have barely started when he gives a cry. "Look, there are some people, two of them on horseback; come on, let's ask them where we are." They shout at the tops of their voices and to their delight the horsemen turn towards them. Running fast Rupert reaches some bushes just as one of the strangers dismounts. "Oh my," gasps the little bear. "Here's another man in olden clothes. Who can he be?"

RUPERT IS MARCHED OFF

"What's this?" the leading man demands.
"Give me that fiddle!" he commands.

The little friends are at a loss
To know what makes those men so cross.

"We've found the fiddle, that is true,
But now we need the fiddler, too!"

The soldiers place the chums between,
And march them off across the green.

Without any further pause both the new strangers stride up the bank towards the young friends. "Oh what gorgeous clothes they have," thinks the little bear. "Oh, look at those wonderful spears. They must be soldiers." The two men, however, pay no attention to Rupert. They march straight to Simple Simon, glare at the fiddle and snatch it roughly from the boy. They move away, though not very far and then stand for some minutes arguing in loud voices while the little pals look on in bewilderment. In a few minutes the soldiers return, and the first man frowns. "We have found the fiddle," he shouts, "but how can we take it back without the fiddler to play it? Come ye both with us. Time presses." "Here, steady on, I'm not a real fiddler!" quavers Simon. "Are ye not?" barks the soldier. "Did I not hear sounds from afar? Protest no more, but come." And with a tall, silent guard on either side Rupert and Simon are marched firmly away.

RUPERT RIDES ON HORSEBACK

"Come," says the leader, "up you get!"
Then on his saddle Rupert's set.

When Simon's on the other horse,
The soldiers choose a woodland course.

The little bear feels ill at ease,
And asks, "Where are we going, please?"

"To serve our king," is the reply,
"We'll reach that castle by and by."

While they are moving forward both Rupert and Simon try to explain how they found the fiddle and how Simon tried to play it to attract somebody's attention when they became lost, and all they want is to get back to Nutwood. Their words have no effect at all on the silent soldiers who walk straight ahead to where their horses are tethered. Then Rupert is lifted on to one horse, Simon on to the other, the soldiers mount behind them and off they trot into a wood.

Soon Rupert speaks again. "I'm sure this isn't the way to Nutwood," he says nervously. "What are you doing with us?" "Peace, 'tis not for me to tell thee everything," says the man gruffly, breaking his silence at last. "The matter brooks no delay. The king may wake at any minute." "Did you say king? What king?" Rupert asks, suddenly very interested. The man says no more and soon they are through the wood. Before them stretches another forest and from it rises a big castle.

31

RUPERT ENTERS THE CASTLE

The four descend on rocky ridge,
Then gain the stronghold by a bridge.

"We found the fiddle, and the bow,
But could not trace the fiddler, though."

The courtier says, "A fiddler small
Is better far than none at all!"

"Our fiddler's gone, without a trace,
But here's a lad to take his place."

The chums almost forget their worry at being lost and they are not frightened, as the big silent men seem quite gentle. Down a steep hill they go and up through the forest until they reach a bridge spanning a gorge beneath the castle walls. A little more climbing and they all dismount outside a doorway, where a young courtier meets them. "We discovered the fiddle but of the truant there was no sign," says the soldier. "Wherefore we have brought the fiddlers who held it."

The young courtier gazes in surprise at Rupert and Simple Simon. "How now? What marvel is this?" he says. "Can you play a royal fiddle? Methinks the king will be startled. However, follow me. Perhaps you will suffice. A small fiddler is better than no fiddler at all." Taking the fiddle and the bow he leads them in and down stone steps. Another figure meets them and Rupert gazes in mounting excitement at the man's striped tunic and strangely shaped fiddle.

RUPERT STARES AT THE FUSS

"That man I met before I came
Had clothes like yours – yes, just the same!"

Above their heads a bell rings out,
"To work! To work!" the fiddlers shout.

"Just find yourselves some place apart!
Our busy time's about to start!"

"Whatever can the matter be?"
Says Rupert. "It seems mad, to me!"

The newcomer looks concerned to see the fiddle and such small people with it. He calls over his shoulder and is joined by another man. At the sight of him Rupert starts forward. "Oo, look at you!" he cries. "There was another man dressed just like you walking near Nutwood. He's gone to see our windmill. Did the fiddle belong . . . ?" Before he can finish there is a loud clanging above his head and all turn to look at the swinging bell. "He is awake! Quick to work, everybody," says a voice.

The sudden clanging of the bell seems to put everyone into a panic. The second fiddler pauses long enough to tell the little pals to go up the steps and find some corner where they will not be in anybody's way, then he hurries off. Upstairs they walk along a corridor and find themselves in a wide hall where there is wild activity. People are rushing about carrying things and shouting to each other. "They seem mad," says Rupert, shaking his head. "What can be the matter?"

RUPERT'S PAL DROPS HIS CAP

"Let's go, before they notice us!"
Gasps Simon, frightened by the fuss.

"Oh, dear! Look where your cap has gone!
I hope it won't get trodden on!"

Then, with a cry the steward trips,
Along the polished floor he slips!

"I hope you haven't come to harm!"
Cries Rupert Bear, filled with alarm.

At the sight of so many people running about Simple Simon becomes very nervous. "We were told to get out of everybody's way," he whispers. "Let's go." "Yes, but where?" says Rupert. "We don't know our way about the castle." "Oh anywhere away from here!" says Simon, grabbing Rupert's arm and scuttling through some curtains and down a passage. "Half a mo'," calls the little bear. "Your cap has blown off." He pauses and looks back just as a steward appears following them through the same curtains. Rupert goes to pick up the cap, but he is just too late. The steward, who is rather stout, is carrying a dark box on a cushion that prevents him from seeing exactly where he is going, and catching his foot in the cap he lurches forward. In his anxiety to save the box he falls awkwardly and skids along the polished floor. Then he sits up and stares at Rupert. "Why, who be ye?" he demands. "I know you not. Did you cause my fall?"

34

RUPERT CARRIES THE BOX

"My ankle's hurt! Oh, lackaday!"
The steward gasps in great dismay.

"The king is waiting! I must ask
You, little bear, to do this task."

"He must be served at any cost,
There's not a moment to be lost!"

Then through the curtains Rupert goes,
He must not drop that box, he knows.

Hearing the bump Simon returns and picks up his cap. At the sight of yet another the plump steward looks more bewildered and tries to get up. "My ankle! 'Tis wrenched. I cannot rise," he cries. "Oh dear, can we help you up?" asks Rupert. "Nay, there is no time," groans the steward, pointing to the box on the cushion. "His Majesty has need of these and on the instant. I cannot take them. Who now can bear them to him? Are you strong and can I trust you?"

Rupert offers to go back to the hall to fetch help, but the steward will not hear of it. "The matter brooks no delay. Not a moment must be lost," the man declares. "His Majesty must be served and at once. You must do it. Quick, away with ye!" He points to another curtained doorway. He sounds so urgent that Rupert dare not ask what is in the box. Picking up the cushion and box very carefully he turns, and while Simon holds the curtains back he passes into the room beyond.

Rupert and the Fiddle

RUPERT FEELS VERY NERVOUS

He marches forward, all alone,
To where the king sits on his throne.

The kindly monarch isn't vexed,
"Well, well!" he laughs. "What marvel next?"

"A little bear, forsooth!" he beams,
"My steward likes to jest, it seems!"

He puffs out clouds of fragrant smoke,
And heartily enjoys the joke.

Once through the curtains Rupert finds himself in a vast and lofty room. At one side is a high round balcony and at the far end is a richly clad figure on a couch. He wears a black crown and his round face breaks into a jovial smile when Rupert approaches. "Well, well, what marvel now?" he cries. "Do my eyes deceive? Instead of my faithful steward there cometh a little *bear!*" Rupert is so nervous that he can find no words, and only watches while the other, still smiling broadly, opens the box and takes out two jewelled objects that he fits together to make a handsome pipe. "Well-a-day, mercy me," he chuckles. "Am I not a lucky monarch to have such courtiers! They are forever devising new whimsies to delight me. A little bear, forsooth! 'Tis a goodly jest indeed." Soon he is puffing clouds of fragrant smoke. "Now, my little courtier, be at ease," he says with a merry laugh. "Let me have the full story. Whence come you to my castle?"

RUPERT SOON UNDERSTANDS

Three more march in to serve the king,
A table, bowl and straws they bring.

"My pipe and bowl! 'Tis well, so far,
But tell me where my fiddlers are!"

"Your fiddlers three? Your pipe and bowl?
Then you must be – yes! – Old King Cole!"

Just then, a frightful whining sound
Makes Old King Cole turn sharply round.

Before Rupert can answer the curtains part and three men march solemnly into the great room. The first is carrying a small table, the second a bowl, and the third is holding two drinking straws. Very carefully they place these objects near the couch for their master's approval. The monarch inspects their work. "So far 'tis well," he says. "I have my pipe and now you have brought my bowl, but where are my fiddlers three?" At the last words of his companion Rupert gives a start and looks at him. "Did you say your pipe and your bowl and your fiddlers three?" he gasps. "Then you must be . . . oh, please, are you really Old King Cole?" "Aye, of course I am," smiles the monarch. "How came you to enter my castle without knowing that?" "But you don't look very old," says Rupert. "Ah, little flatterer, perchance 'tis being so merry that keeps me young," chuckles the king. At that moment they hear an extraordinary noise echoing through the gallery.

RUPERT GASPS IN AMAZEMENT

His pipe goes tumbling from his hand,
He gasps, "'Tis more than I can stand!"

"Go, stop those fiddlers! Fetch them in!
They shall explain this frightful din!"

"I've heard that awful noise before!"
Breathes Rupert, then it stops once more.

"Why, Simon!" cries the little bear,
"Whatever are you doing there?"

As the weird noises from the gallery get worse King Cole puts his fingers into his ears and in his agitation he drops his jewelled pipe. Rupert hurries to pick it up and to his relief it is not damaged. Meanwhile the attendants have sprung into action as the king issues his orders. "Go, stop those fiddlers three," he shouts. "Hale them hither into my presence. This must be explained. Why make this abominable noise instead of the gay melodies with which they are wont to please me?"

Rupert waits beside the king as the attendants run to the gallery. "That noise was just like the one I heard when this adventure started," he says. "Only it sounded worse because it was so much louder." At length the curtains part and in comes the procession, three figures, to stand before the king. Two of them are fiddlers dressed in striped tunics; and to Rupert's astonishment the third is a small person. "Oh, it's Simple Simon!" he cries. "Hi, Simon. What are you doing there?"

"The fiddlers said they needed me
To make their number up to three!"

"Please, Simon only did his best!"
And Rupert quickly tells the rest.

"We took him to replace our third,
Who left today, without a word."

"I think your fiddler went away
Because he wants a holiday."

Simple Simon looks very unhappy. "They wanted three fiddlers," he says. "No one knows where the third fiddler is, so they made me come in and play." "I might have known it was you making that terrible noise!" cries Rupert. Turning, he introduces Simon to the king and at last he can explain the finding of the fiddle in the hollow tree and how he and the boy came to be at the castle. Gradually the king's face broadens into its usual merry smile. The men put down their instruments.

"Your Majesty wishes for fiddlers three," says the eldest. "The third could not be found so we . . ." "Yes, yes, I know where he is!" says Rupert in excitement. "Please, I'm sure I saw him near my home. He said he never had any holiday and he was taking one towards Nutwood. He's looking at our windmill." The king's smile becomes even broader. "Little bear, you have enlightened me," he murmurs. "Holidays forsooth! Why did I not think of that?"

RUPERT WAVES GOODBYE

"So holidays are what they need!
Then I'll arrange some, with all speed!"

"Go quickly! You must help to track
My missing man, and bring him back!"

"If only Simon could have come,"
Says Rupert, waving to his chum.

Then Rupert has a thrilling ride,
Across the sunny countryside.

In a moment all is bustle again as King Cole issues more orders. "My court is a centre of such jollity and merriment that it never came to my mind that my fiddlers might wish a holiday betimes," he declares. "Thanks to you, little bear, the manner shall be arranged speedily. Meanwhile you shall be returned with all despatch to lead the search for my missing man." And taking Rupert outside he points to a horse and rider prepared for his journey home. Rupert is delighted at the work that he has been given and he runs to be lifted on to the soldier's horse. "And where's Simple Simon? Isn't he coming too?" he asks. "Nay not yet," says the king. "First I await the return of the truant. If he cometh not, then your Simon must remain. Methinks a bad fiddler is better than no fiddler at all and, with practice, he may improve." The king and Simon wave goodbye and soon the horse is jogging away from the castle and through the surrounding woods.

RUPERT REMEMBERS THE TREE

"The fiddler went towards that wood,
Let's search down there! I'm sure we should!"

As Rupert speaks, to his delight,
The missing man bobs into sight!

"My fiddle's lost! I can't return!"
The fiddler sighs, in great concern.

"It isn't lost!" calls Rupert. "Look!
You left it in this hollow nook!"

After a long ride Rupert begins to recognise the landmarks and at length he asks the soldier to put him down. "This is about where I saw the man you are seeking," he says. "Look, there's the windmill that he wanted to visit." As he speaks there is a rustle at the bottom of the steep slope near him and next moment the head of the missing fiddler appears above a boulder. "Yo ho, 'tis my little bear again!" cries the man. "And, I declare, one of my king's pikemen, too. This is excellent. I had feared myself lost." The soldier sternly asks the truant why he has been away so long. "In truth I had meant to be well on my way back to the castle by now," exclaims the fiddler. "But affairs have gone awry. Rather than carry my precious fiddle further I hid it for safety in a hollow tree. Now, search as I will, I can find neither tree nor . . ." "Oh please, I know where the tree is," cries Rupert and running to another part of the forest he points it out, and the fiddler follows with expectation.

RUPERT SCAMPERS HOMEWARD

And now, his troubles at an end,
The fiddler calls, "Farewell, young friend!"

Then Rupert sets off at a run,
To tell his Mummy all he's done.

But first, he spies the stoat again,
And stops a moment to explain.

Meanwhile, his pals come into range.
They think his tale is very strange.

The fiddler is horrified to see that his fiddle is no longer in the hollow tree. "Hold, no need for distress," laughs the soldier. "Thy music returned before thee, and a strange new fiddler came with it. This little bear would tell the story, but time presses. We must away to face our king. If we tarry he may lose his merriment." Mounting the same horse they gallop away over the hill. Rupert waits until they are out of sight and then he decides he must scamper with all speed back towards his own cottage. On his way downhill Rupert spies the stoat, and while he is pausing to explain why the mysterious noises have stopped he is overtaken by Bill and Algy and Reggie, who have been following. "Oo, I'm glad to see you chaps," he cries. "I was right. There *was* a queer noise, and I found what it was." He tells the full story and Bill looks excited. But Algy only grins. "So it's Simple Simon and a fiddle and Old King Cole now!" he laughs. "Oh, Rupert, what a yarn!"

RUPERT WANTS TO MAKE SURE

"I'm not quite happy in my mind,
For Simon had to stay behind!"

Next day he tells his startled chums,
"Let's watch to see if Simon comes!"

They think it's just another lark,
Then Bill stops short and whispers, "Hark!"

"It's Simple Simon! I'm so glad!"
Cries Rupert, hurrying to the lad.

Rupert doesn't stop to argue, and hurries to tell his Mummy of the wonderful time he has had at the castle. "The adventure won't be over until I am sure that my pal is safe," he says. "May I go out again tomorrow morning?" Mrs Bear looks doubtful, but at length she consents, and after breakfast he runs and finds Bill and Algy again. "I say, you two, will you come with me to see if King Cole has kept his promise and sent Simple Simon home? I shall not be happy until I know he's all right." Algy stares. "You do stick to your weird story," he says. "Come on, Bill. We may as well humour him." They move off in the direction that Rupert followed yesterday and suddenly Bill Badger pauses. "Hush, I can hear a queer noise myself now," he whispers. "Yes, so can I," says Rupert. "That's it! It's the fiddle again!" The noise comes fitfully and then stops, but, running along together, they reach a glade, and find Simple Simon peeping over a bush.

RUPERT PROVES HIS TALE

"The king says I must learn to play,
To give his men a holiday!"

"A fortnight each? For fiddlers three?
That's six weeks' playing! Goodness me!"

"Yes! I'll replace them, each in turn!
Goodbye! I've such a lot to learn!"

"Your tale was true then, all along!"
Laughs Algy Pug. "And I was wrong!"

"Hello, Simon, so you're safe," Rupert calls. "Did Old King Cole let you bring the fiddle away?" "No, this is another one, an old one," says Simon, looking very happy, "and the king says that if I practise hard and get clever at it I can go and play at the castle for six weeks every year so as to give each fiddler a fortnight's holiday in turn. He never realised that they needed holidays until you told him." "Oo, you *are* lucky!" cries Rupert. "No wonder you look so happy with all the fun to look forward to." Rupert has one last question. "Where are you going to practise your fiddle playing?" he asks. "Oh, my Daddy says that I must practise in our attic whenever he's out at work," laughs Simon, "so I shan't worry any of you! When I play well you shall come and listen to me." And off he goes, while Rupert and Bill and Algy stroll homeward. "So that queer adventure of yours really happened after all," says Algy. "I only wish we could have shared it!"

RUPERT
and the
Green Man

RUPERT RAKES THE AUTUMN LEAVES

When Rupert Bear awakes, he sees
The leaves are changing on the trees.

"If you are going out to play,
Do wear your scarf – it's cold today."

While raking leaves, he hears a sigh,
And then sees Hedgehog trundle by.

"Please would you save some leaves for me?"
Says Hedgehog, rather hopefully.

The leaves have been turning red, orange, yellow and gold. Autumn is finally here! When Rupert wakes up, he sees the autumn leaves scattered all over the ground. "I'd better go and help Daddy rake the leaves," Rupert says to himself. After breakfast, Rupert gets ready to go outside. "You'd better wrap up in your scarf to stay warm," says Mrs Bear. Rupert thanks his Mummy and makes his way outside, where Mr Bear is already on the drive, raking leaves.

Crackle! The dry leaves crunch under Rupert's boots. "There are so many leaves this year!" Rupert exclaims. Mr Bear hands Rupert the rake. Rupert is just wondering whether he will be able to jump in the piles of leaves after they finish, when Hedgehog waddles past. "Hello," Rupert calls down. "Hi, Rupert!" squeaks Hedgehog. "It's going to be a cold winter. Will you put some leaves in a nice, quiet corner of the garden so I can make a cosy nest?"

RUPERT GREETS EDWARD TRUNK

"When winter comes, then I must rest –
These leaves will make a cosy nest."

The birds fly swiftly through the sky
And Rupert hears a chum pass by.

It's Edward Trunk! He wears a grin.
"Hello," calls Rupert. "Do come in!"

"I'm picking produce," Edward tells.
"Oh, please can Rupert come as well?"

Rupert agrees to help out, and he and Mr Bear watch Hedgehog burrow into the pile of leaves. "See you in the springtime," Hedgehog yawns. The wind starts to whistle, and Rupert looks up to see the swallows flying together in a perfect V-shape. "I wonder how they all know when it's time to fly south," he muses. Rupert's thoughts are interrupted by a shout from outside the gate. "Hello, Rupert!" calls Edward Trunk. "Hello, Edward," says Rupert. "Do come in!"

Rupert gives the rake back to Mr Bear, and he and Edward go inside the warm house. Edward says excitedly, "Tomorrow is the Nutwood Autumn Fête. I'm going to Nutwood Common to forage for autumn produce to display at the show." "Oh, Mummy, may I go too?" asks Rupert. "Yes, what a lovely idea," Mrs Bear replies, "I have seen lots of horse mushrooms and rose hips out on the common." She finds a woven basket for Rupert, so he can carry all the produce he collects.

RUPERT CROSSES THE COMMON

They cross the common by the hill.
"Oh, look, it's Podgy!" "Yes, and Bill!"

Says Bill, "I'm glad that we've found you.
We're picking nuts and berries, too!"

The chums walk on and soon they see
The Nutwood Autumn Fête marquee.

They're most excited for the fair,
And find more produce to take there.

With their baskets dangling from their arms, the chums cross Nutwood Common together. Edward tells Rupert to keep a keen eye out for berries or hazelnuts, since those are his favourite autumn goods. Rupert scans the common. "Look over there!" he says, pointing. "I think that looks like Bill Badger and Podgy Pig," Edward answers. Bill waves, and Rupert and Edward stroll over to meet them. Bill shows off his basket. "We've been out collecting produce, too," he says proudly.

As they come down the hill from the common, Rupert spies a giant marquee that has been assembled on the grassy knoll. The great tent is decorated with colourful bunting. "There will be games and prizes tomorrow," Edward says, eagerly. "And food," adds Podgy, "lots of delicious food." Then Bill spots some tall, white horse mushrooms by the trees, and the four friends make their way over. "Mummy was right about the mushrooms," Rupert thinks to himself.

RUPERT MEETS BEN THE BOATMAN

The shrubs and brambles here are thick
With juicy berries, ripe to pick.

Then Edward asks excitedly,
"Is that Ben's boat-house I can see?"

"There's reeds and teasels in the fen
Just down that way," says Boatman Ben.

"The stream is shallow. For your hunt
I think you'd better take my punt."

Soon, the chums come to hedgerows laden with blackberries, raspberries and elderberries. It doesn't take long to fill their baskets with the juicy, ripe berries. They wander further along, listening to the merry warbling of the thrushes and redwings. When they pass the banks of a small stream, Edward gives a joyful shout. "I see a house on the water!" "That's Boatman Ben's house," Rupert explains. "Why don't we go over and say hello to him?"

Ben the Boatman is very happy to see Rupert and his friends. Rupert describes the Autumn Fête and shows Ben what they have found so far. "Do you know," Ben begins, "there are reeds and teasels and rich pickings further down the stream?" Rupert is delighted to hear this, as it will make the perfect addition to their autumn collection. "But how do we get there?" Podgy asks. "I don't want to get wet!" "Take my punt," offers Ben. "The stream is quite shallow."

RUPERT PUNTS DOWN THE RIVER

The boatman helps them with the boat,
And waves to them when they're afloat.

They punt along the stream with ease
And drift beside the blackthorn trees.

"I love sloe berries – what a treat!"
"But Podgy, wait! They're not to eat."

They pass by a peculiar door.
"What could that lead to? Let's explore!"

"I know how to punt," Rupert says, as he takes the pole from Ben and balances on the small boat. "My friend Sailor Sam once showed me." Ben gives a wave, and the others wave back. *Swish! Swish!* They punt down the stream, which is sparkling in the autumn sunlight. "I see sloe berries," says Edward, and Rupert guides the punt towards the blackthorn trees so his friends can pick the berries. "Sloe berries are my favourite," says Podgy, putting a handful in his mouth.

"No, Podgy," laughs Bill. "These are for the fête tomorrow – they're not to eat." Rupert punts onwards, and the river widens. The bank is lined with reeds, swaying gently in the autumn breeze. As the chums drift lazily down the river, Rupert realises they have gone quite a bit further than he thought. "What's that?" he wonders out loud, for the punt reaches a jetty by a curious-looking door. Everyone is eager to explore, and Rupert ties the punt to the jetty so it won't drift away.

RUPERT ARRIVES IN A GARDEN

They leave the boat on solid ground,
And step inside to look around.

The leaves are yellow, gold and green
A place this lush they've never seen!

The garden is a leafy maze.
The chums could all stay here for days!

Cries Rupert, "What's this on the ground?"
He picks up something smooth and round.

Rupert gives the old brass handle a turn, but at first it doesn't budge. "It's stuck – I don't think this door has been opened for a long time," Rupert supposes. "Let me try," offers Edward. Using his great strength, Edward pushes against the door, and at last it creaks open. Rupert gasps in surprise. "What is it, Rupert?" asks Bill, who's standing behind them. "See for yourself," Rupert replies, and the four pals enter. They are inside the richest garden they have ever seen!

The huge leaves are bold colours – red, gold, yellow and green. The plants form a soft canopy overhead, with giant, trumpet-like flowers dangling down from the vines. "This place is like a maze!" Bill marvels. "Let's look around, but we'd better be careful not to get lost . . ." Rupert is walking forwards, but he stumbles on something under his foot. He reaches down and picks up a shiny conker. As he stands up, another conker bounces off his head.

RUPERT DISCOVERS A CONKER TREE

"Look, Rupert! It's a chestnut tree.
Let's try to knock more conkers free."

He looks around and finds a stick,
Then throws it upwards, with a flick.

"Ooh, ouch!" a deep and rich voice cries.
The chums all jump up with surprise.

Then Rupert gasps, for with a creak,
The leafy figure starts to speak!

The pals look up to where the conker came from. "We're right beneath a horse chestnut tree!" Podgy declares. "Shall we have a game of conkers then?" Bill suggests. Rupert thinks that this is a grand idea, so he hunts around until he finds a stick. He tosses it into the foliage, hoping to dislodge a few more conkers. "I think you missed," Bill says nicely, so Rupert finds another small stick to have another go. He takes aim at the horse chestnut tree and hurls the stick upwards.

"Ouch!" a deep, rich voice cries. "W-w-who said that?" yelps Podgy. Rupert looks around nervously and says, "I can't see anyone other than us!" "Do you suppose someone is up there in the tree?" Edward asks. Rupert stands on his tip-toes to get a better look. The leaves are rustling – someone is there! To the chums' alarm, the tree appears to come to life! "Who threw that stick?" the tree-man calls down. "I-I-I did!" stutters Rupert. "I'm very sorry!"

RUPERT MEETS THE GREEN MAN

"I am the Green Man. Do not fear.
I tend these plants all through the year."

"Meet Conker here. When it gets cold,
He makes green leaves turn red and gold."

Then Conker flings a conker. Snap!
He really is a cheeky chap.

The Green Man says, "Come to our den
And Conker may be less rude then."

The tall figure looms out of the vegetation, and says in a kind voice, "There's no need to be frightened. I am the Green Man, and this garden is my home." Rupert searches his memory – he's sure that he has heard legends of the Green Man before! "I look after all the trees and plants throughout the year," the Green Man continues. Then he introduces a tiny figure. "This is Conker. He is the one who changes the colours of the leaves when autumn comes."

Conker is about the size of Rupert's arm, and he looks like a little sprite with a horse chestnut for a head! Rupert is about to introduce himself, but Conker makes a rude noise and flicks a conker at the chums. Rupert and Bill duck, and the nut hits Podgy on the forehead. "Ouch!" Podgy squeals. "I'm very sorry," the Green Man apologises. "Conker is a very cheeky fellow. Why don't we all go inside? Maybe we can keep Conker out of trouble then."

RUPERT GOES INSIDE THE HOUSE

*"I'd never guess that you live there.
Oh, what a place!" says Rupert Bear.*

*The wooden door creaks open wide,
And so the chums all step inside.*

*They marvel, in the entry hall,
At flutes and whistles, big and small.*

*"And when I play my magic reed,
The birds know to fly south with speed."*

The Green Man carries a tall staff, dotted with tiny leaves. He ushers the chums along a grassy path, lit by shafts of sunlight. As they approach a large, stone house, Rupert gives a start. "Is that where you live? I never would have guessed!" he says in awe. The Green Man smiles and opens the tall, wooden door to invite the chums in. The hallway is huge, with high ceilings and a thick carpet along the ground. The walls are lined with strange-looking reeds and pipes.

"What are these?" asks Bill. "They look like musical instruments." The Green Man gives a chuckle. "Indeed they are," he replies, and he plucks down a smooth wooden pipe to show them. "This reed is my favourite. When I play my autumn melody, the birds hear it and know that it's time to fly south before the winter." "Yes!" cries Rupert, as he suddenly remembers the birds he saw that morning. "I was wondering how they all knew when to go!"

The kindly Green Man serves up tea,
And eyes their produce thoughtfully.

"We're going to the Nutwood Fair –
We will show off our produce there."

The Green Man muses, "If I may,
I'll give you more goods to display."

Then Conker smirks at the Green Man.
He has a very naughty plan!

Rupert is just starting to feel thirsty, and fortunately the Green Man offers the chums a drink. They sit down at the small wooden table together, and the Green Man beams when he looks down at the baskets that Rupert and his friends are carrying. "What lovely autumn produce!" the Green Man says proudly. "We've collected it for the Nutwood Autumn Fête," Edward explains. He has a flyer for the fête, so he hands it to the Green Man. "What fun!" the Green Man cries.

The Green Man steps out of the room, but returns a moment later with a flat basket brimming with vibrant dahlias, begonias and ferns. "These are some of my favourite autumn plants. Why don't you take them with you for the Autumn Fête?" Edward tucks the new basket under his arm. The chums are so busy thanking the generous Green Man that they don't take any notice of Conker, who is wearing a big smirk. Conker has had a very naughty idea!

RUPERT HAS MORE TROUBLE

He turns two chums to leaves, and then
He will not change them back again.

"There is no need to feel alarm –
The Spring Imps can reverse the charm."

The Green Man, to the chums' relief,
Soon conjures up a magic leaf.

The leaf floats swiftly, and they bring
The small leaves to the Imps of Spring.

Flash! There is a bright light, and suddenly Bill and Podgy grow smaller and smaller . . . until they're no longer Bill and Podgy, but a pile of autumn leaves! While Rupert and Edward look on in disbelief, Conker dances around, giggling. "Oh dear," the Green Man sighs. "I expect Conker thought it would be funny if he turned your friends into autumn leaves." "But what will happen to them?" Rupert asks anxiously. "You needn't worry," the Green Man advises.

"Take your friends to the Spring Imps," the Green Man continues. "They will be able to change them back." Rupert is relieved. "In fact," the Green Man adds, sternly, "I think Conker had better go along. The Spring Imps can have a word with him about his cheekiness." Rupert thanks the kindly Green Man and gathers up the baskets. "How will we get to the Spring Imps?" asks Edward. The Green Man smiles and conjures up a magic leaf to take them there.

RUPERT FINDS THE SPRING IMPS

"Oh, Spring Imp, please do make amends.
These leaves aren't leaves – they are my friends!"

The Imp's enchantments change them back.
They reappear then, with a CRACK!

"Oh dear! We're in each other's clothes!"
How did this happen? No one knows!

The Imps tell Conker to behave,
And off the chums go, with a wave.

The magic leaf carries Rupert, Edward and Conker all the way to where the Nutwood Imps of Spring live. Rupert calls out and one of the Imps comes out from their underground home by the giant tree. "Please will you help us?" Rupert asks, after he explains the situation. "These leaves are really Podgy and Bill!" Rupert has been carrying the leaves very carefully, and now he hands them over to the Imp. "Everyone stand back," the Imp warns.

Crack! There is another flash of light, but this time the leaves grow larger and re-form into Rupert's pals! Rupert is comforted, but Edward starts to laugh. "Look – you're in each other's clothing!" he chuckles. "Oh dear," sighs the Imp. "Something about my spell didn't go *quite* right . . ." Still, the chums are very glad to be back in their bodies, and they thank the Spring Imps. As they wave goodbye and walk back over the common, they hear the Imp scolding Conker.

RUPERT'S MUMMY IS AMAZED

At home, the little bear regales
His Mummy with his thrilling tales.

He hears a noise and looks outside.
Is that the Green Man in his stride?

As morning comes, he cannot wait
To take his produce to the fête.

"I see the marquee over there.
Let's go inside," says Rupert Bear.

That night, Mrs Bear tucks Rupert up in bed, and he tells her all about his adventures. "Well!" she marvels. "What a thrilling day you've had!" Rupert is excited about the Autumn Fête tomorrow. "Please may we go?" he begs. "I don't see why not," she replies. "I can't wait to see the autumn flowers on display." Later, Rupert hears a soft noise outside his room, so he peeps out of the window. Although it's dark, Rupert thinks he sees a tall, leafy figure tiptoeing past . . .

The next morning is the day of the Nutwood Autumn Fête. Rupert and his Mummy and Daddy put their coats and scarves on. Rupert takes his basket of produce from the table, where he left it the night before. "Is everyone ready? Then let's go," says Mr Bear cheerfully. It is another sunny, autumn day, and there is a feeling of excitement in the air when they arrive at the marquee. "Why don't you run ahead and find your chums," Mrs Bear tells Rupert.

RUPERT ATTENDS THE NUTWOOD FÊTE

Inside the big tent, on display,
Are fruits and berries, reeds and hay.

Concealed amongst the plants and trees,
A leafy figure Rupert sees.

"Hi Podgy!" Rupert says with glee.
"Let's play with conkers, you and me."

A conker hits him. "Ouch!" he cries.
"Oh, not again," poor Rupert sighs.

Rupert goes ahead and joins the crowds inside the marquee. Inside, he sees a huge display of plants and greenery. There are tables loaded high with autumn berries and vases of flowers. In one corner, Rupert notices a leafy green display. As he looks closer, Rupert can't believe his eyes. He is sure that the display winked at him! Rupert smiles back, but before he can say anything, he hears someone calling his name. "Hello, Rupert!" It's Podgy Pig.

"Look at the display over there – can you see anything?" Rupert asks Podgy. "No, what is it?" Podgy replies. "Never mind," Rupert laughs, when he realises the Green Man has disappeared into the leaves. "Shall we have a game of conkers?" Podgy agrees, and Rupert takes out the conkers he gathered in the Green Man's garden yesterday. They play for a while until a conker bounces off Rupert's head, and he hears a familiar giggle from up in the trees. "Oh no – not again!" Rupert sighs.

Spot the Difference

Rupert has made two new friends today! There are 10 differences between these two pictures of Rupert meeting the Green Man and Conker. Can you spot them all?

RUPERT
and the
Gardens Mystery

John Harrold.

RUPERT IS ASTONISHED

One sunny morning, Rupert spies
A sight that makes him rub his eyes . . .

"Whatever can the matter be?"
His father asks him. "Come and see!"

Out in the garden, it seems that
Someone has crushed the spring bulbs flat . . .

"Look!" Rupert cries. "I think I've found
A mark that's been left on the ground . . ."

One morning, just before Easter, Rupert is woken by a shaft of golden light, streaming into his room. "It's going to be a sunny day," he thinks and throws open the window. As he looks out, he gives a cry of astonishment and hurries off to wake his parents. "W-what's the matter?" blinks Mr Bear as he pulls on his dressing gown and stumbles out on to the landing. "It's the garden," Rupert cries. "Something terrible's happened. Come and see . . ."

Following Rupert into the garden, Mr Bear soon sees why his son was so surprised . . . All the spring bulbs, that looked so wonderful the day before, have been trampled into the ground, as if someone has been marching about in the flower beds! "Who can have done such a thing?" he gasps. "I don't know," says Rupert. "I didn't hear anything during the night . . ." Then he breaks off and points to something he's spotted in one of the flower beds.

RUPERT FINDS A CLUE

"A footprint! But who left it there?
It seems so odd!" gasps Mr Bear.

"Come on!" he says. "We'd better go
And let Constable Growler know."

The Constable is puzzled too –
He doesn't quite know what to do . . .

Then Mrs Pig appears. Can she
See Growler very urgently?

"Good gracious!" gasps Mr Bear as he looks at what Rupert has found. "It's a footprint of some sort, although I can't imagine what kind of creature made it!" "Whatever it was must have crushed all the flowers," says Rupert. "That's right!" murmurs Mr Bear. "I don't like the look of this at all! Come on, Rupert. We'll get dressed, then tell Constable Growler what's happened. If this creature's as big as it seems, then it could be dangerous . . ."

PC Growler is as puzzled by the strange footprints as Rupert and his father. "Never seen anything like this before . . ." he mutters. "I wonder if it could be those Fox brothers up to one of their silly pranks?" "Surely they wouldn't have trampled all over our flowers?" says Mr Bear. "That would be too much, even for them!" Before Growler can reply a voice calls his name and Mrs Pig appears at the garden gate. "Thank goodness I've found you," she cries.

RUPERT HEARS MRS PIG'S TALE

"My daffodils were trampled flat,"
She starts to tell him, "Just like that . . ."

"Our garden here was ransacked too!
That's why I came to look for you . . ."

"Thieves!" Growler cries. But no, she found
A monster's footprint on the ground!

Her tale is interrupted when
Young Gregory arrives just then . . .

"What's wrong?" asks PC Growler. "It's my garden," declares Podgy's mother. "When I woke up this morning all the daffodils in my flower bed had been trampled to the ground . . . just like these!" "Dear me!" exclaims the policeman. "I don't suppose you saw any sign of what did it?" "No," replies Mrs Pig. "But the door of our garden shed was left wide open, with everything strewn all over the lawn . . ." "Thieves, eh?" says Growler and reaches for his notebook.

"Oh, no!" cries Podgy's mother. "You don't understand. It wasn't thieves who trampled down the daffodils: it was some sort of terrible monster. We found a giant footprint in the corner of the flower bed . . ." "So did we!" says Mr Bear. "Rupert found it, next to the trampled bulbs . . ." At that moment, Gregory Guineapig comes running into the garden. "Constable Growler!" he calls. "My mother sent me to find you. Something dreadful's happened!"

RUPERT LISTENS TO MRS GUINEAPIG

His mother's had a dreadful fright
"Our garden's been wrecked in the night!"

"My tablecloth's been stolen too,
I dread to think by what or who!"

"The Monster!" Rupert cries. "I'm sure
We'll find that it has struck once more!"

"Don't worry!" Growler says, "I'll go
And find out what my colleagues know . . ."

"It's something to do with your garden, isn't it?" asks Rupert. "Yes," gasps Gregory. "But how did you know?" Rupert has just started to explain about the mysterious trail of footprints when Mrs Guineapig arrives in a terrible tizzy. Something has trampled all over her prize tulips . . . "That's not all!" she adds as the others listen attentively. "Whatever it was pulled down my washing line and made off with my best linen tablecloth!"

PC Growler doesn't know what to make of such strange goings on! "It must be the same creature," says Rupert. "Its footprints were found in all three gardens . . ." "I know!" groans the policeman. "But I have no idea what sort of animal we're looking for. Trampled bulbs, ransacked sheds, and now . . . missing tablecloths! It's all very peculiar. I think I'd better telephone my colleagues in Nutchester," he declares. "Perhaps they'll know something about it . . ."

RUPERT SPOTS THE 'MONSTER'

Soon afterwards the Bears all hear
A whistling sound from somewhere near . . .

They hurry to the gate and see
As strange a sight as there could be . . .

A hidden creature of some kind
Runs past, with Growler close behind!

He orders it to stop, but on
The creature runs, until it's gone.

Deciding that there's nothing more to be done, Gregory and his mother make their way home, together with Mrs Pig. "I still can't imagine what sort of creature trampled all over our flowers!" says Rupert's mother. Suddenly, a shrill whistling sound fills the air. "That's Constable Growler's police whistle!" cries Rupert. "It sounds as if he's coming this way . . ." He runs to the garden gate, together with his parents, then gives a startled cry . . .

"Look!" exclaims Rupert. "Good gracious!" cries Mr Bear, "Whatever's that?" Speeding towards the cottage comes PC Growler, in hot pursuit of a strange, tall creature, wrapped in some sort of sheet. "Stop!" cries Growler, but the hidden creature runs on with giant strides and vanishes off across the common. "It's no use!" puffs the exhausted policeman, stopping to take off his helmet and mop his brow. "It's just too fast for me to catch!"

RUPERT'S MOTHER HELPS GROWLER

*"I chased it from the high street, where
It upset everybody there . . ."*

*"Good gracious!" Rupert's mother cries.
"That cloth is one I recognise!"*

*"The missing cloth?" gasps Growler. "Then
That was our 'Monster' once again!"*

*"It might be dangerous! I'll go
And let the Nutchester men know . . ."*

"W-what were you chasing?" Rupert asks Growler. "I don't really know!" shrugs the policeman. "I was on my way back to the station, when I suddenly heard a cry of alarm. As soon as I reached the high street I saw that . . . that *thing* bump into poor Mr Anteater, then knock over the whole of the greengrocer's display. That's when I blew my whistle and started to give chase . . ." "It . . . it was wrapped in Mrs Guineapig's tablecloth!" declares Mrs Bear.

"Are you sure that was Mrs Guineapig's cloth?" asks PC Growler. "Yes," says Rupert's mother. "I'd recognise it anywhere . . ." "Then this must be the creature that wrecked everyone's gardens!" the policeman declares. "But why should it hide under a tablecloth?" asks Mr Bear. "I don't know," says Growler. "Perhaps as a disguise? Whatever the creature is, it could be dangerous. I want everyone to keep away from the common, while I go and telephone Nutchester."

RUPERT FOLLOWS GREGORY

Rupert decides to go and tell
Young Gregory the news as well.

"Can't stop!" his chum declares. "You see,
I've got my painting things with me . . ."

"How strange!" thinks Rupert. "I'm quite sure,
That Gregory can't even draw!"

He follows Gregory to find
Just what his chum has got in mind.

After Growler has left, Rupert decides to go and tell Gregory all about the mysterious creature. Avoiding the common, he takes the long way round to his chum's house and spots the little guineapig, going out for a walk. "Wait for me!" he calls. To Rupert's surprise, Gregory is carrying a paintbox and a jar of water. "I . . . I'm on my way to do some sketching," he declares and hurries off without another word. "How strange," thinks Rupert. "I didn't know Gregory liked painting."

"I wonder what he's going to paint?" thinks Rupert as he watches Gregory hurry away. "He's certainly carrying a paint box and a pot of water, but where's his sketchbook?" Overcome with curiosity, Rupert decides to follow his chum to find out what he's up to. At first nothing unusual happens, then Gregory stops and peers all round. From his hiding place behind an old tree, Rupert sees him turn off the main path and disappear up a narrow farm track . . .

RUPERT LEARNS GREGORY'S SECRET

*"A ruined barn! But why was he
So keen to come here secretly?"*

*As Rupert peers around the door
His pal lifts something from the straw . . .*

*"A huge egg!" Rupert gasps, but he
Is overheard by Gregory.*

*"What egg?" he cries, attempting to
Keep it well-hidden, out of view.*

Following Gregory up the narrow track, Rupert finds that it leads to an enormous ruined barn. He is just in time to see his friend prise open the barn door and slip inside . . . "I wonder why he's being so secretive?" thinks Rupert and tiptoes up the path to take a closer look. As he peers round the open door, he spots Gregory, rummaging about in a heap of straw. "Good!" he cries. "It's still here." To Rupert's amazement, he pulls out a huge egg!

Unaware that Rupert is watching, Gregory rests the egg on top of an old packing crate then turns to open his paints. "I say," cries Rupert, "that's the biggest egg I've ever seen." "Who? What!" squeaks Gregory. "Oh, it's you, Rupert. Fancy creeping up on me like that!" "I'm sorry," says Rupert. "I only wanted to see what you were painting. Wherever did you get that enormous egg?" "What egg?" says Gregory, standing in front of the box.

At last he explains how he found
The huge egg lying on the ground . . .

"I want to paint it straightaway
To show you all on Easter Day!"

"But Gregory, it must belong
To someone. Taking it is wrong!"

As Rupert speaks, the two pals see
The egg start moving suddenly . . .

"Don't be silly!" says Rupert. "I saw the egg when you took it from under the straw . . ." "You can't have it!" cries Gregory. "I found it. It was lying in our vegetable patch!" "I don't want to take it," laughs Rupert. "I only want to have a closer look." "Oh, all right," says Gregory. "But it's meant to be a surprise. I'm going to paint it bright colours and have the biggest Easter egg in Nutwood. You won't tell any of the others, will you?"

"Of course not," says Rupert, "but where did the egg come from?" "I just told you," says Gregory. "Yes," says Rupert. "But what sort of creature could have left it there in the first place? It won't be very happy if it comes back and finds the egg's gone. If I were you, I'd put it back straightaway." "Shan't!" squeaks Gregory. "It's my egg now, and I'm going to paint it." Just then, the pals hear a strange tapping sound as the egg begins to move . . .

RUPERT TAKES THE EGG BACK

Gregory tries to run away,
But Rupert says they've got to stay.

"Before the egg begins to crack
Let's see if we can put it back."

He carries the egg nervously.
What will the baby creature be?

As they arrive, the startled pair
Are shocked to see what's standing there . . .

"Help!" cries Gregory and runs towards the door. "Come back!" says Rupert. "We can't just go off and leave the egg to hatch out in an empty barn. Whatever's inside will be frightened and need help . . ." "But it could be anything," cries Gregory, nervously. "Come on," says Rupert, picking up the egg as gently as he can. "Show me the exact spot in your garden where you found the egg and we'll put it back there to hatch out safely . . ."

On the way back to Gregory's house, Rupert hears the tapping grow louder and starts to think of all the things that might have laid such an enormous egg . . . It can't have been an ordinary bird, so perhaps it was an alligator, or a giant snake, or even a fire-breathing dragon . . . "We're nearly there now," says Gregory, breaking in on Rupert's thoughts. The pair turn into Gregory's garden but have only gone a few paces when they stop and stare at what lies ahead.

The Monster's back, and seems to be
Searching the garden thoroughly . . .

Replacing the egg carefully,
The two pals turn around and flee!

The pair keep running until they
Are certain that they've got away.

As Growler sees them run along
He stops and asks the chums, "What's wrong?"

There, in the middle of the Guineapigs' vegetable patch, stands the same strange creature which PC Growler chased through the middle of Nutwood earlier that morning. "It's come back!" gasps Gregory, "only this time it's trampling our vegetables . . ." "Quick!" whispers Rupert. "I don't think it's noticed us yet." Putting the egg down on the soft grass, he grabs Gregory's hand and marches him back along the garden path before the creature looks up.

The moment they are clear of the garden, Rupert and Gregory take to their heels and run to fetch help as fast as they can. "W-what if it follows us?" wails Gregory. "Don't worry," says Rupert. "I'm sure it was too busy with the vegetable patch to have seen us . . ." As they race round the corner, the pair are relieved to see PC Growler, strolling towards them. "Hello," he smiles. "You two seem in a bit of a rush. Whatever's the matter?"

*"The 'Monster'!" Rupert gasps. "We saw
It trampling down more plants, I'm sure . . ."*

*"I'll deal with this!" says Growler. "Though
You'll need to show me where to go . . ."*

*"I've asked an expert from the zoo
To come and tell us what to do."*

*"Look!" Growler cries out in surprise,
Unable to believe his eyes . . .*

At first Rupert is too out of breath to say anything more than, "The . . . the monster! It's come back . . ." "Monster?" asks Growler. "You mean the thing I chased along the high street?" "That's right," nods Gregory. "It's in our garden again, trampling on the vegetables!" "This calls for firm measures!" says Growler, producing his truncheon. He tells Gregory to go and wait at the police station, while Rupert shows him where the creature's lurking . . .

On the way to Gregory's garden, Growler tells Rupert the police in Nutchester have promised to send someone from the local zoo to have a look at the mysterious footprints. "I don't suppose you saw what the creature was?" he adds hopefully. "No," says Rupert. "It was still covered by the tablecloth." "Not a sound!" whispers the policeman as they near the garden gate. "We'll try to creep up on it." The pair peep cautiously into the garden, then reel back in surprise . . .

RUPERT SEES THE EGG HATCH OUT

*"An ostrich!" he gasps. "And I see
It's an egg as well. Bless me!"*

*Then, as the startled pair draw near,
They see an ostrich chick appear!*

*The mother ostrich spots the pair
And fixes Growler with a stare . . .*

*"Don't move!" warns Rupert, but too late –
She starts to charge towards the gate!*

"An ostrich!" gasps Rupert. "Look! It's all tangled up in Mrs Guineapig's tablecloth." "So that's the mysterious creature!" cries Growler. "No wonder its footprints looked so strange . . ." The huge bird pays no attention to the newcomers, but peers attentively at the egg, which Rupert left lying by the side of the path. The tapping sound from inside the egg grows louder and louder, until, suddenly, the shell cracks and out pops a tiny ostrich chick . . .

"I hope the zoo chappie gets here soon!" says PC Growler. "I'm not sure I fancy trying to take these two into custody." As he speaks, the mother ostrich looks up and glares at him crossly. "Don't make any sudden moves!" warns Rupert, but it's too late. Stepping forward, to place herself between her chick and the strangers, the ostrich flaps her wings then charges up the path. "Watch out!" cries Growler. "She's coming this way . . ."

RUPERT MEETS A ZOOKEEPER

The pair retreat, but as they do
They spot a lorry from the zoo.

The keeper goes across to say
"Hello" to Olive straightaway . . .

"A baby ostrich! Goodness me!"
He smiles and strokes it tenderly.

He hands Rupert the chick and then
Says, "Time we got you home again."

As Rupert and Growler back away from the angry ostrich, they hear a lorry coming along the road towards them. It stops and a man in a zookeeper's uniform hops down from the cab. "They said in the village I'd catch you here," he smiles. "Looks like I'm just in time!" Walking towards the ostrich, he raises his cap and greets her like a long lost friend. "Hello, Olive," he calls. "No need to get excited. I'm sure these two gentlemen don't mean any harm . . ."

"Well, I never!" smiles the keeper as he spots the ostrich chick in Gregory's garden. "What a splendid little fellow. You must be very proud." The mother ostrich seems quite content as he picks up the chick and hands it to Rupert to hold. "We'll take you both home now," the keeper adds gently. "You can ride in the back of the lorry, while young Rupert here looks after your chick." The ostrich smiles approvingly and follows him back to the van.

RUPERT GOES TO THE ZOO

"Goodbye!" waves Growler, glad to see
That things have ended happily.

"It's just as well the 'Monster' you
Discovered had come from our zoo!"

"The reason Olive had to stay
Was someone took her egg away . . ."

Then, as a set of gates appear
The keeper says, "We're getting near!"

When everything is ready, and Olive is safely aboard, the zookeeper drives off, leaving PC Growler to go and tell Gregory it's all right to come home. "I thought it might be Olive the moment I heard about your mysterious footprints," the keeper tells Rupert. "She went missing from the zoo a couple of days ago and nobody knew where she'd gone . . ." "Why did she run away?" asks Rupert. "And why ever did she make such a mess of everyone's gardens?"

"Olive probably got a bit bored," explains the keeper. "I wouldn't be surprised if she simply wanted to see more of the outside world . . . The thing that puzzles me is why she spent so long searching all those gardens. It's almost as if someone took her egg and hid it somewhere where she couldn't find it!" Rupert says nothing but thinks of Gregory and the ruined barn . . . "Never mind!" says the keeper as they near the zoo. "She's almost home now . . ."

Inside the zoo, Rupert can see
The animals all wander free . . .

They stop outside a tall hut where
The ostrich lives – "She likes it there . . ."

They wave goodbye to Olive, then
Drive back to Nutwood once again . . .

"My Easter egg!" sighs Gregory.
"The biggest one I'll ever see . . ."

Inside the zoo gates, Rupert is amazed to find a large park, full of lots of different animals, all roaming as they please. "No bars and cages here!" smiles the keeper. "Look! There's Olive's house." He stops the lorry outside a tall hut with a thatched roof. The ostrich seems delighted to be home, and soon leads her little chick inside. "Talking of homes, it's time you were getting back to Nutwood," the keeper tells Rupert. "Come on, I'll take you there."

When the zookeeper arrives in Nutwood, he drives straight to Mrs Guineapig's house to apologise for what happened to her tablecloth. "Don't worry!" she says. "I'm only sorry that the poor ostrich got so badly tangled up in it . . ." "I don't suppose you've got any more big eggs?" asks Gregory, picking up a piece of the broken shell. "I'm afraid not," smiles the keeper. "Just as well!" laughs Rupert. "Who knows what might hatch out next?"

HOW RUPERT MAKES A PAPER LILY

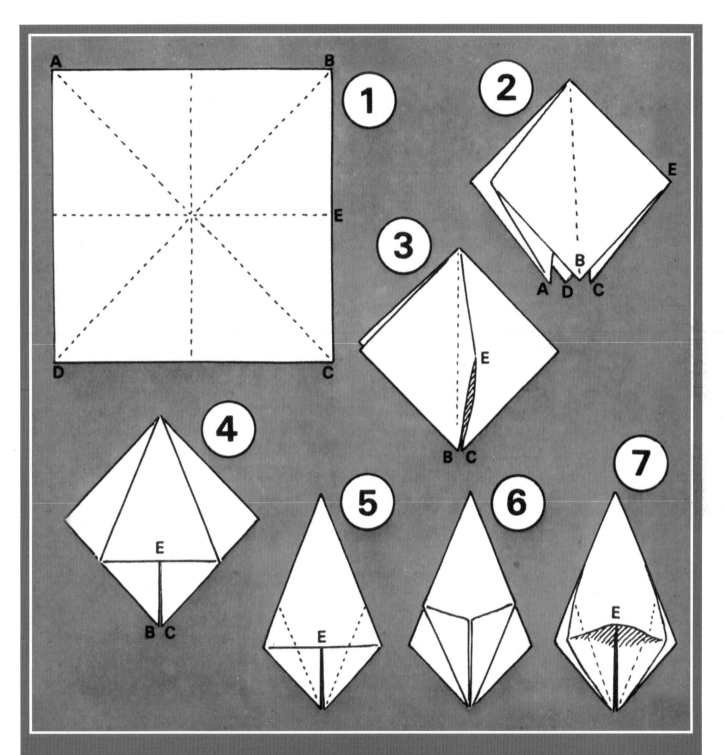

Take a square of thin paper and fold opposite corners together both ways, then turn it over and fold opposite sides together both ways, then turn it over and fold opposite sides together to make the pattern of creases in Figure 1. Now bring the four points together (Figure 2), lay the paper flat so as to leave E sticking up as in Figure 3 and press E down so that it lies exactly on the middle line (Figure 4). Repeat this with the other three sides to make Figure 5. Using the dotted lines shown in Figure 5 fold the lower sides to the middle (Figure 6) and open them out again. Now comes the only tricky bit as you lift the flap at E (Figure 7) and, using the creases just made, carry E right up, slowing and carefully, until you can press the sides down as in Figure 8. Repeat this all round and it must be done very neatly. Don't hurry.

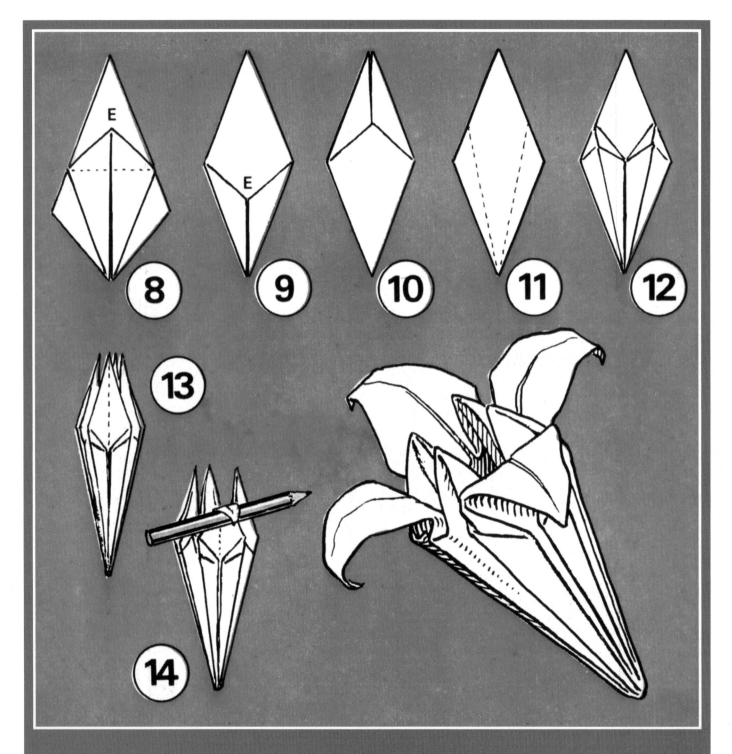

Then fold down the point at E and the other three similar points (Figure 9). Turn the whole thing the other way up (Figure 10), open it at a plain face (Figure 11) and again fold the lower sides to the middle by the dotted lines (Figure 12). Repeat this all round and press down as hard as you can. Some of the folds are now rather thick so the model is sure to open a little as in Figure 13. Lastly take each point in turn and bend it outwards. An even better way is to roll it over a pencil, as in Figure 14, again treating each point in turn. The large drawing shows how the finished lily should look. Try it with pink or orange paper. If you make several lilies you can arrange a cluster of them in a small plastic pot, adding a few sprigs of fern or other greenery, and they will look very nice as a decoration for your bedroom.

RUPERT

"The gale has blown all these tiles down,"
Says Algy with a worried frown.

All night it has blown a fearful gale. Now Rupert goes out to see the damage. When he comes to Algy Pug's house he finds his chum glumly filling a barrow with tiles blown off his roof. When Algy says he must dump the tiles somewhere Rupert offers to push the wheelbarrow. Bingo, the clever pup, has the same problem – what to do with bits blown off his workshop. "Put them in Algy's wheelbarrow," says Rupert, "and we'll look for a place to dump them."

and the GEMLINS

Poor Bingo, too, is in distress.
The gale has left his shed a mess.

"Dame Tansey's house is worst of all,"
Says Bingo. "We had better call."

The pals decide that it will have to be outside the village and on their way out of Nutwood they come across Dame Tansey's cottage. It really has suffered in the gale and the chums find the poor old lady weeping. "Oh, dear," she wails. "Windows broken, shutters damaged, tiles blown off, fence knocked down. It will cost so much to mend I won't be able to buy coal for my stove."

Then he says, "I know how to do
Repairs to fence and shutters, too."

RUPERT AND HIS CHUMS HELP OUT

Young Algy's help is quite enough,
So Rupert goes to dump the stuff.

At length he finds the very spot
To dump the rubbish he has brought.

He tips the rubbish carefully
Into the hole left by the tree.

Then as he turns back, out it shoots
From somewhere underneath the roots.

"We must help the old lady in some way," Rupert whispers to the others. "I'm sure Algy and I could do some repairs," pipes up Bingo. "Rupert can find somewhere to dump all the broken stuff." The other two eagerly agree and Dame Tansey starts to brighten up at once. So while Algy and Bingo set about putting the house to rights Rupert sets off with the wheelbarrow. He hasn't gone far when he comes across a tree that has been blown down in the gale. "Whew!" he gasps.

"What a hole it has left . . . hey, that's the very place to dump this rubbish!" He trundles the heavily laden barrow to the edge of the hole. Yes, it really is a big hole. Just the place. He tips the barrow and sends the broken tiles and splintered wood into the hole. He steps back rather pleased with himself and almost at once gives a yelp of alarm. For all his rubbish comes hurtling back out of the hole and he has to duck to avoid being hit by it. "What on earth's happening?" he cries.

RUPERT MEETS A GEMLIN

A man in miner's clothes peers out
And shouts, "Hey, watch what you're about!"

"Down there's our diamond mine, young bear.
How dare you dump your rubbish there!"

"Our diamond mine's deep underground.
Now you are here, I'll show you round."

The miner seals the entrance tight,
And Rupert feels a twinge of fright.

In the next instant there is a scrambling noise from the hole and a small, very angry face appears out of the darkness. It belongs to a little man who is wearing a miner's helmet with a lamp on it and holding a pickaxe. He tosses out the pickaxe and climbs after it. "How dare you throw your nasty rubbish down our diamond mine!" he shouts. "D-diamond mine?" exclaims Rupert. "I'd no idea there was a mine of any sort here. Oh dear, I am sorry!"

The little man's frown fades: "I think you really are sorry." He pauses. "Didn't know there was a diamond mine here, eh?" he muses. "Well, now you're here would you like to see it?" "Oh please!" cries Rupert. "Right, then down you go," the little man laughs and ushers Rupert into the hole. Rupert finds that he is standing on a steep flight of steps cut into the earth. "Just a moment," says the man and while Rupert watches he blocks the entrance with a rock. This worries Rupert a bit.

At length they reach a sort of cage
To take them down to the next stage.

Into the lift and down they go
Towards the diamond mine below.

A truck stands on a railway line.
"Jump in! We'll soon be at the mine."

"I say," cries Rupert, "this is fun!"
As down the railway line they run.

The little man sees that Rupert is worried. He smiles: "Don't be frightened. I just want to make sure no one else discovers the mine." He leads the way down and down until they come to a low tunnel that leads to a brightly lit chamber where a lift is waiting. They enter the lift, the man pulls a lever and slowly it begins to descend. Rupert's worries have quite gone now. "I say, this mine of yours must be awfully deep," he exclaims as the lift keeps going down.

"Pretty deep," the little man chuckles. "But here we are." The lift stops and they get out and at once climb into something that looks like a tiny railway truck. Indeed, it is standing on narrow rails that disappear down a gentle slope. "This will take us down to where the real mining is done," the man explains. "Now hold tight." A brake is released and with a rumble the truck starts to move, gathering speed as it rattles downwards. "Oh, this is fun!" laughs Rupert.

RUPERT STARTS BACK BY BARGE

"We Gemlins mine a special gem,
Black diamonds – our King treasures them."

"Are those black diamonds?" Rupert blinks.
"Looks more like coal to me," he thinks.

Now to the palace it is borne,
And turned to gems that can be worn.

Rupert is told to leave by barge,
And finds himself alone in charge!

As the truck rumbles down the slope the little man explains, "I'm what's called a Gemlin. We're called that because we mine for gems, you know." Just then the truck comes to a stop in a well-lit gallery and Rupert sees lots of little men like his guide chipping at the rocky walls with pickaxes. The stuff they are mining is dumped on a moving belt. "I say, it looks just like coal!" Rupert bursts out. "Nothing of the kind!" retorts his guide. "The mine belongs to our King and what we're mining here are black diamonds." The little man leads the way beside the moving belt until they come to an underground river where barges are being loaded with the black lumps. "They're on the way to the palace to be made into gems," he explains. "Well, thank you," Rupert says. "Now I'd better get back. My pals will wonder what's happened to me." "Then step aboard," smiles the Gemlin and ushers Rupert on to an empty barge nearby.

RUPERT LOSES CONTROL

*"You'll reach two tunnels. You must take
The left-hand one. Make no mistake."*

*Now Rupert poles his way along
Helped by the current, fast and strong.*

*"Those are the tunnels," he decides.
Towards the left the barge he guides.*

*But though he tries with all his might,
The current pulls him to the right.*

"B-but how do I get back on a barge?" Rupert wants to know. "Simple," says the Gemlin. "Use this barge pole to punt your way downstream." He smiles when he sees that Rupert is uncertain. "It really is quite easy," he says. "You'll soon get used to it. Just remember that when you come to two tunnels you must take the left-hand one. You'll find a path beside it that will take you back to near where we met." And so Rupert pushes off and although at first he is rather nervous he soon finds that he is getting used to poling the heavy barge along. At last, ahead of him, he sees the two tunnels. There is daylight at the end of the left-hand one he has been told to take. The other, which has a crown above it, leads into darkness. "Whew! I must admit I'm rather glad to see daylight again," Rupert thinks and he pushes hard to steer the barge to the left. But nothing happens. The stream is flowing much faster and he cannot control the barge.

RUPERT GOES THE WRONG WAY

"I must go left at any cost!"
And then, oh, dear! His pole is lost!

There's nothing he can do to shift
The vessel from its headlong drift.

Upon a jetty three guards stand.
"Help!" Rupert cries. "Please help me land!"

"Quick! Get ashore!" one Gemlin snaps.
"Then you'll explain yourself perhaps!"

"Oh my! This is awful!" Rupert gasps as he pushes harder and harder against the pole. Then just when he thinks he is getting the barge to go to the left a swirl of water catches it. The heavy vessel swings sideways and in trying to keep his balance Rupert lets go of the pole. He grabs at it in vain for it is already out of reach. Now he is thoroughly scared. He crouches on the stern of the barge and watches the dark right-hand tunnel getting nearer and nearer.

Next moment he is enveloped in darkness with only the swish of the water to tell him he is still moving along. Then he gives a great sigh of relief for ahead he can see a gleam of light that gets bigger and brighter until the barge sweeps out into a cavern that is brightly lit. Just inside it is a jetty and on it is standing a group of little men. Rupert doesn't have to shout for help for as the barge nears the jetty the little men catch it with spear-like boathooks and pull it in.

RUPERT MEETS THE GEMLIN KING

"You must have come down here to spy!
You'll pay for this!" the Gemlins cry.

On Rupert now the guards take hold
And cry, "Our ruler must be told!"

Sternly the King says he must know
What Rupert's doing here below.

But when he's heard the story through,
He says, "I do believe that's true."

The faces Rupert finds himself looking into are anything but friendly. He is dragged out of the boat by two of the little men. Before he can even begin to explain, the third of his captors shouts, "Spy! You have come to spy on us. Oh, the King shall hear of this!" And Rupert finds himself bundled up steps which lead to a narrow path skirting a cavern. He tries to explain about losing the barge pole but is told to be quiet. At last he notices that the light is brighter and he feels carpet under his feet. He looks up. And there, ahead of him, perched on a throne is the King of the Gemlins. He listens to the guards but unlike them he also listens to Rupert, and when the little bear finishes his tale, rises and gazes at him. "You look honest," he says at last. "Perhaps you did drift here by mistake. But now you are here and I must decide what is to be done with you." "Oh, please," Rupert starts to say. "Quiet!" shouts a guard.

RUPERT IS OFFERED A GIFT

"Come, little bear!" Then Rupert's led
Into a room that lies ahead.

"You cannot work down here, it's clear.
You're far too tall for us, I fear."

"Black diamonds are made into things
Of beauty – bracelets, brooches, rings."

The treasure chest is opened. "Pray,
Choose what you'd like to take away."

Rupert's knees are shaking as the Gemlin King stands deep in thought. Then the little monarch steps down from his throne and beckons to Rupert to follow him. He leads the way to a low archway of jagged rock and strides through, then turns and watches Rupert. "Hm, I thought so," murmurs the King as Rupert has to stoop to follow. "Had you been small enough to walk straight through you could have stayed and joined my Gemlins. But you're too big." "Thank goodness," thinks Rupert.

"Pity," says the King. "I'm sure we'd have got on well. Now, follow me!" And a very puzzled Rupert hurries after him and finds himself at last in another cavern where Gemlins are making jewellery from the black diamonds. "This is where we store our black diamond treasure," the King says. At his command a huge treasure chest is opened. It is full of brooches, necklaces and rings. "Now, little bear!" cries the King. "You may choose a gift to take home with you!"

RUPERT MAKES A CHOICE

He thinks of Poor Dame Tansey's plight
And asks, "Plain lumps, please, if I might."

"The storekeeper!" a guard is bid,
And bangs his spear upon a lid.

"Now storeman, hark to what I say.
Some plain black lumps to take away."

A length of rope is handed out.
"Now pull!" The storeman gives a shout.

Rupert lifts a sparkling black necklace from the treasure chest and is admiring it when he suddenly remembers what Dame Tansey said about not having enough money left to buy coal. "Oh, please, your Majesty," he says, "would it be possible for me to have instead some ordinary lumps of coal – er, I mean black diamonds – for a friend of mine?" "You know, I have heard it called coal before," says the King. "But only we Gemlins can make black diamonds from it."

"But if that's what you want . . ." He leads the way to where lids are set into the floor and tells a guard, "Summon the storekeeper!" The man taps on one of the lids and up pops a grimy face. "Ho, storekeeper!" commands the King. "Prepare some black diamond chunks for this little bear to take away." "At once, sire," says the man and he pulls out a rope which he hands to Rupert. "Just hold on to that for a moment, young sir," he asks and pops back into the hole.

RUPERT SAYS GOODBYE

On Rupert's rope a sack is tied.
He feels the heavy lumps inside.

"Upon my word, I do declare,"
The King says, "you're a thoughtful bear!"

"Oh," Rupert cries, "I thought you would
Know, as a bargeman, I'm no good!"

"A bargeman will escort you back.
Just hand aboard your heavy sack."

Rupert wonders what is happening down below as he stands holding the rope. At length he feels a tug on it and the storekeeper calls, "You can pull it up now, young sir." On the end of the rope is a small, but surprisingly heavy, sack. "It must be a sack of coal!" Rupert exclaims. Then he remembers and corrects himself: "Of course, I mean black diamonds. Oh, and how pleased Dame Tansey will be with it!" "You're a thoughtful little bear to help a friend so," the King says as he leads the way back through the tunnels. At last they come out on the landing stage where Rupert arrived. But what a difference. This time the guards stand respectfully to attention. When he sees an empty barge waiting for him Rupert is dismayed. "Your Majesty, as you know, I'm not much good at managing barges." The King smiles. "Don't worry," he says. "This time one of my best boatman will go with you." And so Rupert hands his sack to the boatman and climbs aboard.

RUPERT SETS OFF ALONE

"Farewell!" As Rupert's visit ends,
He's sad to leave his new-found friends.

The other tunnel isn't far.
"Right!" says the bargeman. "Here we are!"

"Now you must walk, if you don't mind,
And climb the flight of steps you'll find."

As Rupert sets off on his own,
He wishes he were not alone.

The kindly little King is sad to see Rupert go, and as the barge moves off he calls, "Farewell, little bear! I wish you could have stayed!" And Rupert, who feels quite glum himself, almost wishes that he could, and cries, "Thank you, your Majesty, and goodbye!" The return journey is upstream and as Rupert watches the Gemlin boatman having to use all his strength to push the barge against the current he realises he could never have made the journey on his own.

At last, though, the barge reaches the entrance to the tunnel Rupert should have taken earlier. Skilfully the Gemlin steers the craft into it and moors beside a very narrow path. "This is where you get out, young sir," he tells Rupert. "I have to turn back now." Feeling just a bit uneasy, Rupert puts his sack ashore and scrambles after it. "What do I do now?" he wants to know. "Oh, it's easy," replies the Gemlin. "Just follow this path until you come to some steps." So off Rupert sets again.

RUPERT GETS OUT OF THE MINE

At last he finds a long, steep flight
Of steps which rise towards the light.

He spies the fallen tree below:
"That's good! Now my way home, I know."

The little bear climbs down the hill,
And groans, "Here's all that rubbish still!"

The entrance is so well concealed,
Its secret will not be revealed.

Rupert now begins to realise just how heavy the little sack of coal really is as he trudges along the waterside path. It is much longer than he expected and after a while he wonders if somehow he has missed the steps he has been told to look out for. Then suddenly there they are and Rupert heaves a sigh of relief. But the hardest part of his return journey lies ahead for now he has to climb as far as he came down in the lift. But just when he is about to give up he sees daylight ahead and in a moment is out in the open looking down on the fallen tree where his adventure began. He is relieved to see that Algy's wheelbarrow is safe and he scrambles down to it. Of course, he realises with dismay, the rubbish is still there too. "Oh well," he tells himself, "I shall just have to load it back into the barrow and find some other place to dump it." Then he peers into the hole under the tree. The mine entrance is so well sealed no one would guess it was there.

RUPERT IS HELPED

"Oh dear," sighs Rupert. 'This is grim."
Just then a car stops close to him.

"It's the Professor's servant. Hi!
What luck that you should just chance by!"

The little servant lends a hand.
"Oh thanks!" says Rupert. "This is grand."

"We'll tip the rubbish in my car.
I'll dump it later. There we are!"

Exhausted after his long climb back to the surface, Rupert stands gazing at the rubbish which is scattered all around. "It makes me even more tired just looking at it," he mutters. "But I suppose I had better get it into the barrow and find some other place to dump it." Just then a car horn sounds and Rupert turns to see the little servant of his friend the old Professor. "Hello, young Rupert," calls the little man. "You look pretty glum. What's wrong, eh? Lost your way?"

Then he spies all the rubbish. "I say, you didn't scatter this mess, did you?" "Of course not," Rupert says and starts to explain how it comes to be there. This leads him into telling about his adventure and as he talks the little man helps him to gather up the rubbish and dump it in the back of his little truck. "I'll get rid of it for you later," he promises. "I'll find a place where it won't bother people. Now would you like a lift?" "Very much, thanks," Rupert says.

RUPERT ASKS THE PROFESSOR

The servant hears his story through,
Then begs, "Please tell my master, too."

"Please," Rupert asks the kind old man,
"Tell me what this is if you can."

"Give me a lump, it would be best
To put it through a special test."

"This super kind of coal will blaze
For many months," the old man says.

As they bowl along the country lanes on the way to Nutwood, the little servant gets Rupert to tell him again about the black diamonds and how the Gemlins were able to make it into jewellery. "Amazing, amazing," the servant repeats. "Do you know, I'm sure my master would like to hear about this and maybe have a look at the black diamonds you've brought back." "Why, of course," Rupert says. And in a little while the old Professor is greeting his young friend warmly and inviting him into his castle home. They go straight to the Professor's workroom and Rupert does not spend time telling his story again but simply hands the Professor a piece of black diamond from his sack. "Can you tell me what this really is?" he asks. The old man examines it very closely then exclaims, "It is coal, but a sort I've never seen before. We must test it!" He heats a bit of it in a small furnace then puts it in a sort of cauldron. "Remarkable!" he gasps.

RUPERT IS BACK WITH HIS PALS

"A very small amount will last
Until the winter is well past!"

"Dame Tansey will be pleased, it's plain,"
Thinks Rupert, setting off again.

"Oh good!" exclaims the little bear.
"Algy and Bingo are still there."

Says Rupert, "I've been busy too.
I've something strange to show to you!"

"What's remarkable about it?" Rupert wants to know. "Don't you see?" the Professor cries. "It keeps glowing brightly and leaves absolutely no ash. It's quite amazing stuff. Never seen any coal like it. It's quite clear it will go on burning for months. May I keep this piece?" "Of course you may," Rupert agrees. "There's plenty left for Dame Tansey. And since it lasts so long it will save her lots of money." Then he loads the sack into Algy's wheelbarrow and sets off for

Dame Tansey's cottage. From some way off he sees that his two pals are still working around the cottage. "Hello, Rupert!" Bingo greets him. "Where have you been? It's taken you ages. In fact, we've almost finished the repairs, haven't we, Algy." "Indeed we have, you old slacker," Algy laughs. "Not at all," Rupert says. "Just you wait till you hear my story and see what I've brought for Dame Tansey!" "Come on then, let's see it!" Bingo cries.

RUPERT AND HIS PALS GO HOME

The three decide to lay a fire.
Just sticks and paper they require.

Dame Tansey can't believe her eyes.
"A bucketful of coal!" she cries.

The poor old lady's thrilled to learn.
For months and months her fire will burn.

Of all her worries she's quite free,
Thanks to the thoughtful Nutwood three.

Algy and Bingo can't believe their ears when Rupert tells them what the old Professor has said about the black diamonds. "Come on, let's try it then," says Bingo who always likes to know how things work. And so while Rupert tips the black diamonds into a bucket his pals collect paper and sticks to make a fire. They are ready to fill the grate when Dame Tansey returns. "A bucketful of coal!" she marvels. "Why, I haven't been able to afford coal for weeks." "But this is a very special sort of coal," laughs Rupert and he asks her to light the fire. In a very short while the fire is crackling away merrily and Dame Tansey sits wide-eyed and smiling at Rupert's promise that the coal will last for months. "Oh, my!" laughs the old lady. "You've all been so good, repairing my house and giving me this wonderful coal, thank you, thank you!" Later as the friends leave Dame Tansey's house Bingo says, "Come on now, Rupert, you're going to tell us the whole adventure!"

RUPERT
and the
SNOWBALL

Freddy and Ferdy Fox soon wish they had not thought of a snow prank to play on Rupert and Algy. Ferdy's plight is worse than his brother's, but luckily a clever bird befriended by Rupert comes to the scene just in time.

RUPERT IS FORCED TO SHELTER

"The weather's clearing! I'm so glad!"
Says Rupert. "What a week we've had!"

"Yes," Mummy smiles, "you may go out,
But take some buns, and move about."

"There's Algy!" Rupert Bear exclaims,
"Now we can have some splendid games!"

The two chums shelter from a squall,
Then – "Crar-rk!" – there comes a dismal call.

It has been a hard winter. Snow and yet more snow has been falling, and Rupert has been kept indoors until he is tired of playing with his toys, and he knows all his books by heart. One morning the sky seems to be less dark overhead, and he runs to his Mummy. "The weather's clearing," he declares. "May I go for a run in the snow?" "Very well, perhaps it will do you good," Mrs Bear smiles. "Mind you move about and keep warm." And she puts a couple of buns in a paper bag for

him to take. The snow underfoot is fairly hard, and Rupert is soon scampering about. "Hello, there's Algy Pug over there," he murmurs. "Hi, Algy! Are you tired of staying indoors too? What shall we do?" As the two pals meet, an extra heavy squall of snow forces them to shelter behind a tree. Almost at once Rupert turns. "Hush, someone's calling for help," he whispers. "I hear a voice, but I don't believe it's a person at all," says Algy in a startled voice.

RUPERT FEEDS A HUNGRY BIRD

Once more the plaintive cry is heard,
And now they spy a big, dark bird.

Then Rupert tosses down some crumbs,
"Poor crow, he's hungry! Here he comes!"

"He snatched the bag straight from my hand!"
Gasps Rupert. "I don't understand!"

"He knew you kept the buns in it!
A clever trick, you must admit!"

The dismal sound comes again, and the two pals move towards it through the squall. Next minute they hear it quite near, and they spy a dark object on a branch. "Why, it's a sort of crow," exclaims Rupert. "You poor thing! You do sound miserable. What's wrong? Are you too cold to fly?" "Crar-r-rrk." "Perhaps it's just hungry," Algy suggests. So Rupert tosses crumbs from one of his buns into the snow, and the crow glides down towards them.

"You were quite right, Algy," says Rupert. "The poor crow was starving." He puts his hand into the paper bag to break off some more crumbs when there is a "swoosh", and before he knows what is happening the bird has snatched the bag and is gone. "Well, would you believe it?" gasps the little bear. "That's a jolly clever bird," says Algy. "It knew what was in the bag. But where has it gone?" The last snow has fallen, and they gaze around without seeing the bird.

RUPERT PREPARES SOME SCRAPS

"I'll have to ask for two more buns!"
Calls Rupert, and away he runs.

He dashes home to tell his tale,
Then gasps, "That bird is on my trail!"

"All right!" exclaims the little bear,
"I'll fetch some food, if you wait there."

"He'll do that trick again, perhaps!
I'll fill these paper bags with scraps."

Rupert and Algy wait awhile without seeing anything more of the crow. Then they give up. "Let's make our snowman later on," says Algy, "and I'll bring something to put on it." "Right-ho," Rupert agrees. "Now I'll go and ask my Mummy for some more buns." He hurries homeward, not noticing who is coming after him until he begins to tell Mrs Bear how he lost the paper bag. Then he starts, and points. "Look, I do believe that's the very bird that played the trick on me, Mummy!" The crow flies around close to the cottage. "You want some more crumbs?" mutters Rupert. "Very well!" He fetches a case from the shed and the bird immediately perches on it. "Yes, you're a clever bird, right enough," smiles Rupert. "Now we'll see if you'll show my Mummy the same trick as before." Running into the cottage he collects all the small paper bags he can find, then he busies himself cutting up all the scraps of food that Mrs Bear can spare.

RUPERT STARTS ON A SNOWMAN

Yes! One by one, the crow collects
Those little bags, as he expects.

They watch until no bags remain,
Then Rupert hurries out again.

"Oh, Algy! What a funny hat!
Why ever are you wearing that?"

"It's for our snowman!" Algy cries,
"And I've two buttons for his eyes!"

When the little bags are filled and screwed up Rupert puts them on the case and he and his Mummy watch from the window. As he hoped, the bird goes straight for them, and carries them off one by one. "Well, he is clever!" gasps Mrs Bear. "I wonder why he wants so much. It's too early for nests and little crows. Perhaps he has lots of brothers and sisters." "I don't know, but he's certainly grown fond of me!" laughs Rupert. Then Mrs Bear gives him more buns, and he runs out to find Algy again. Algy has turned up punctually. "What on earth are you wearing?" cries Rupert. "It's a hat and a walking stick for the snowman," laughs Algy. "And I've got two spare buttons in my pocket. Where do we start?" "Somewhere where he can be seen," suggests Rupert. "What about building him at the top of this long slope?" "Oo, no," says Algy. "I'm too tired to enjoy climbing. I vote we build him here." So they both set to work.

RUPERT GIVES A SUDDEN WARNING

"He's perfect, with his hat and stick!"
Laughs Algy Pug. "We have been quick!"

Then Rupert gives a startled cry,
And points towards the slope near by.

A great white ball rolls down the hill!
Each moment it grows bigger still.

Then – whoosh! – the snowball hurtles through,
Just missing them, their snowman, too!

Rupert and Algy build carefully and steadily, making the base wide and strong, and stopping the head when they cannot reach any higher. Then they put in Algy's two buttons for eyes and a bit of wood for a nose, and dab on more snow at the sides to make arms, poking the walking stick through one of them. Rupert has stepped away to admire the snowman, and Algy is putting on the finishing touches, when the little bear gives a sudden shout and points up the long slope.

At Rupert's urgent call, Algy turns to see what has caused his excitement. From very high up the slope behind the snowman, a large white ball is rushing down towards them. Faster and faster it comes, growing bigger and bigger as it picks up more snow, until it hurtles through between the two startled pals, just missing their new snowman. In their fright they both topple over. "W-who could have sent that down?" quavers Rupert shakily. "There's no one in sight up there."

103

RUPERT AND HIS PAL RECOVER

"It's huge!" exclaims the little pup.
"It's made me feel quite shaken up."

"The question is, who sent it down?"
Says Rupert, with a puzzled frown.

"Let's make a snowman from that ball!
We'd do it in no time at all."

"How topping, Algy!" Rupert grins.
"I say, then we'll have snowman twins!"

The sudden arrival of the huge snowball has shaken both the little pals. Looking after it, they see that it has rolled to a stop up another slope in front of their snowman. "My, isn't it a whopper!" exclaims Algy. "Who could have made such a large snowball?" "It's come a good way," says Rupert, gazing up the first long slope. "It's been picking up snow all the way, and may have been small when it started. The question is, who sent it down?" The two friends wait and stare about, but all is quiet.

There is no sign of anyone else, and no more snowballs come down the slope. Algy recovers from the shock and grins. "I've had a lovely idea," he says. "That huge snowball had lots of snow in it. Why shouldn't we use it to make *another* snowman? It would save us half our trouble." "Good idea!" says Rupert. "Let's try." He leads the way, but before he reaches the snowball he pauses in his track as if something has surprised him.

Rupert and the Snowball
RUPERT BACKS AWAY QUICKLY

A muffled noise makes Rupert pause.
He wonders what can be the cause.

Then, as the startled chums step back,
That monstrous ball begins to crack!

"Oo-oh!" cries Algy in alarm,
"I just saw something like an arm!"

"Why, Freddy!" gasps the little bear,
"However did you get in there?"

Seeing Rupert pause, Algy asks what is the matter. "Hush, listen," whispers Rupert. "I can't hear anything," says Algy. But Rupert has crept close to the snowball and holds up a finger for silence. Then he backs away rapidly. Next minute they both hear a muffled noise from inside the ball. "Here, I'm scared!" cries Algy. "Is it going to go off bang?" And, as they watch, the ball quivers, lumps of snow fall away from it, and cracks appear. Instead of going up with a bang the big snowball collapses into large pieces, and to the astonishment of Rupert and Algy the pieces still move as though being pushed by something inside. Screwing up their courage the two pals draw nearer inquisitively, just as a shape like a foot is thrust out of the snow. Algy takes fright and backs away again, but Rupert stops and stares as a head and two dark ears are pushed upwards. "Why, surely it's Freddy Fox!" he exclaims. "What *are* you doing inside that snowball?"

RUPERT FOLLOWS THE TRAIL

"My brother Ferdy! Where is he?"
The little fox asks anxiously.

"I've something awful to confess,
We meant to smash your snowman, yes!"

"But I fell off the sledge, you know,
And rolled down here in all that snow."

"We'll look for Ferdy, while you rest,"
Calls Rupert Bear. "That would be best."

For some minutes Freddy Fox crouches in the snowball, dazed and gasping. "Where's my brother Ferdy?" he wheezes. "How should we know?" replies Rupert in surprise. "Where should he be? In another snowball?" Freddy struggles wearily to his feet and shakes himself and walks a few steps. "Ferdy and I saw you making this snowman," he says, "and we thought it would be a jolly good lark to run into it and knock it down, but I fell off." "Fell off *what*?" demands Rupert. Freddy Fox goes on explaining. "Ferdy and I were on a sledge, high up that slope," be says. "He must have swerved, throwing me off, and as I rolled I must have picked up more and more snow." "You certainly did!" cries Rupert. "There's only one way to see where Ferdy went and that's to go up the slope." He starts climbing, while plump Algy puffs along behind him as fast as he can. "It's fine of you two to help," says Freddy. "I feel too shaky to climb."

He finds the spot where Freddy fell,
The sledge marks are quite clear as well.

"Freddy fell off as Ferdy swerved.
The sledge marks here are sharply curved!"

The sledge marks turn off course once more,
And Rupert wonders what's in store.

He stops abruptly, horrified,
And summons Algy to his side.

Rupert struggles up the slope that is sometimes very steep and sometimes has deep snow into which he sinks. He follows the track that was made by poor Freddy Fox until the snowman is just out of sight, and there he finds what he is expecting. By the time Algy has breathlessly joined him the little bear is looking at a broader mark at the top of the track. "This must be the spot where Freddy fell off and started rolling," says Rupert. "See, those other marks must be Ferdy's sledge marks."

The two pals gaze at the track in the snow. "Ferdy must have swerved very suddenly," says Rupert. "Perhaps he hit a bump under the snow. No wonder Freddy was thrown off, if he wasn't expecting it." "Yes, but where's the sledge now?" mutters Algy. "The marks of the sledge runners are clear enough; let's follow them," says Rupert. They hurry forwards more easily down the new slope until Rupert stops abruptly. "Something terrible has happened!" he cries.

RUPERT WORRIES ABOUT FERDY

"The track leads to the very edge,
So Ferdy's down there, with his sledge!"

"We must tell Freddy straight away,
And start a search without delay!"

The chums are very scared indeed.
They flounder back at their best speed.

"Oh, Freddy's gone off on his own!"
Says Rupert, in an anxious tone.

Algy joins Rupert, and both pals stand horrified, realising what the tracks in the snow mean. "Ferdy must have been going so fast that he couldn't stop, and he went straight over the cliff," whispers Rupert. They lie down and gingerly peer over the edge. "There are big trees growing right against the rock," says Algy, trembling. "D'you think he's in them?" They call again and again without getting any answer. "Come on!" Rupert rises gingerly. "We must go back to Freddy and start a proper search for Ferdy." Rupert leads the way as fast as he can down the track made by the snowball. Though the snowman is standing just as it had been when they started climbing there is no one else in sight. "Where's Freddy Fox?" says Algy. "Has he gone home?" They look around and call him, but as before, there is no answer. "There are some footmarks going off to the right," says Rupert. "He must be searching for Ferdy. Let's follow him."

Rupert and the Snowball

RUPERT SEARCHES THE WOODS

"I'll run for help! I'm sure I should!"
Cries Algy. "You search through that wood!"

The little bear at once agrees,
Then makes his way towards the trees.

"I'm underneath that cliff just here,
So Ferdy must be somewhere near."

"Crar-rk!" The crow calls from a bough.
Gasps Rupert, "What does he want now?"

Algy is not sure whether Rupert's idea is the right one. "If poor Ferdy really went over that cliff with his sledge he must be in awful trouble," he says. "Don't you think I'd better try to find someone to help while you go round towards that cliff?" Rupert agrees, and they separate, and he follows Freddy's footmarks to the right. Soon the marks veer off leftwards. "That direction won't do," he murmurs. "It leads away from those trees at the foot of the cliff." So he decides to go on alone.

Rupert pushes on into the wood, and listens for any noise that may show where Ferdy is. The cliff goes on for some distance, and he looks carefully. Then he stops to think. "I must have walked past the place where that sledge came over the edge," he thinks, "but there's no sign of anything having fallen into the snow below. What can have happened to it?" As he pauses, a loud squawk near by makes him jump. "I do believe it's that clever crow again!" he thinks.

RUPERT DRAGS A HEAVY BOUGH

"He's leading me, there's no mistake!
He's showing me which way to take!"

"There's something hidden in this tree!
Is that what he is showing me?"

"This fallen bough is nice and strong,"
Thinks Rupert, dragging it along.

He hoists his 'ladder' into place,
Then clambers up at his best pace.

When it finds the little bear looking at it, the crow makes a louder noise than ever. "Oh dear, I can't understand that language," Rupert mutters. At that the crow flies away and he watches it, but before long it wheels back to him, and then flies back in the same direction. "I do believe the clever thing wants me to follow," he thinks, and he plods forward. Sure enough the bird perches on one of the trees, and Rupert gazes upwards in growing excitement. "There is something hidden high in the branches!" he gasps. "Whatever is it?" He cannot quite make out the shape of the object, but the bird is now flapping around, and will not move from the tree. "I must climb up there and see what's the matter," decides Rupert. He searches in the snow until he finds a strong bough that has fallen, and, with much puffing and blowing, he hoists it against the lowest branch. "Now for it!" he says, as he clambers up the bough and reaches for a higher branch.

"The bough has slipped! I'm just in time!"
Breathes Rupert, as he starts to climb.

"It's Ferdy Fox! The crow was right!
Just keep calm, Ferdy! Hold on tight!"

"He's dazed! He didn't hear me call,
And if he moves, he's sure to fall."

The little bear is glad to find
His friend the crow, perched close behind.

Rupert is no sooner safe in the lower branches of the tree than he hears a soft thud, and looking down he sees that the big broken bough by which he climbed has slipped and fallen back into the snow. "Oh dear, that's my way of escape gone!" he breathes. "I do hope Algy will not be long in following me." The way is now easy because there are so many branches and he quickly makes his way up to the dark shape. With a thrill he recognises that it is indeed the missing pal Ferdy Fox, caught in the branches. "Hello, Ferdy," he calls. "Aren't you the luckiest fox that ever was! After that terrible fall the tree has caught you and held you as if you were in an armchair!" He waits for an answer and then stares more closely. "He's not listening!" he gasps. "He's had a shock. If he moves while he is so dazed he'll drop right down to the ground. Oh dear, I . . ." A hoarse sound interrupts him as once again the crow alights on a near branch, just above him.

"Crar-rk!" calls the bird, then flutters round,
As if to say, "Look what I've found!"

"The sledge! So this was where it went!"
Gasps Rupert in astonishment.

He tugs the sledge with all his strength,
And gets it firmly wedged at length.

The crow then perches on the board,
And helps him to untie the cord.

Rupert gazes at the crow. "You've been jolly clever and useful so far," he says. "Now we're in proper trouble. I need a bit of rope to tie Ferdy to the tree in case he wakes up and falls. Oh, if only you could understand what I'm saying!" To his surprise the bird squawks once, and flutters to where the branches are thicker. "Yes, there's something else there," mutters Rupert as he follows. "What is it? Surely it can't be . . . ! Yes it is. It's Ferdy's sledge caught in the same tree and still hanging here!" Rupert is now excited. "No wonder there was nothing to be seen at the foot of the cliff!" he cries. "Both Ferdy and his sledge were caught up here." He swings the sledge around until he wedges it firmly in a fork of the branches to take its weight off the strong cord, and quickly begins untying a knot. The bird watches wisely for some minutes, then hops down to undo the other knot with its beak. "Well, you really are a clever crow," says Rupert.

RUPERT FALLS INTO DEEP SNOW

Then Rupert back to Ferdy goes,
He must not take too long, he knows.

The cord is long enough, he finds,
So to a bough his chum he binds.

"This little branch is just the thing.
It bends quite well, so down I'll swing!"

But – snap! – he has no chance to jump,
And tumbles down, with such a thump!

At length with the bird's help, both knots are undone, and leaving the sledge wedged so that it cannot fall Rupert winds the cord over his arm and carefully turns round to make his way back. To his relief he can see Ferdy Fox still lying in the other part of the tree. "Thank goodness he hasn't tumbled," he murmurs as he climbs across. There is enough cord to go twice around his pal's body, and soon Ferdy is secured to a branch while the crow looks on feeling almost as anxious as Rupert.

"There," says Rupert thankfully. "Now Ferdy cannot drop out of the tree when he wakes up. But he'll get jolly cold if he stays long. I wonder if Algy has succeeded in finding anyone." Descending to a lower branch he hears Algy's voice not far away. "Hooray, I'll go and meet him," thinks Rupert. "The bough I used as a ladder has gone, I'll try to swing down on this smaller one." Alas, the little branch won't carry his weight. It snaps, and next minute he is on his back in the snow.

RUPERT'S CHUMS BRING HELP

Says Algy, "I've found help for you!
Here's Rollo, and his uncle too."

Cries Rupert, "I'm so glad you've come!
Oh, please climb up and help my chum!"

"Run, Rollo, run, fast as you can!
Bring me some rope!" commands the man.

"We've found your brother!" Freddy's told,
When he arrives, so tired and cold.

Finding he has not hurt himself Rupert turns over just as his pal reaches him. "What are you playing at?" calls Algy breathlessly. "Is there any sign of Ferdy? Look, I found Rollo and he has asked his uncle to come and help us search." Rupert scrambles to his feet. "But there's no need to search any further," he cries. "Ferdy and his sledge landed near the top of this tree! I've tied him so that he can't fall, but I wasn't strong enough to do anything to bring him down."

Rollo's uncle makes Rupert tell him just what he has been able to do for Ferdy and his sledge. Then he turns to the boy. "Hurry back to our camp," he says, "and bring a length of strong rope while I climb up to this poor little fox." With a slight spring he manages to grasp the lowest branch and swing himself into the tree. A few minutes later Freddy Fox trudges forward. "I heard voices and hoped it was you," he sighs. "Is there any sign of Ferdy?"

114

RUPERT USES THE CLEVER BIRD

Then Rupert tells how he was led,
And shows the crow perched overhead.

"That bird will soon fly off, I hope,"
Says Rollo. "Then I'll use this rope!"

"It's known just what to do, so far,"
Says Rupert. "Come on, here you are!"

Up with the rope the crow then flies,
"I've got it!" Rollo's uncle cries.

Rupert quickly tells the dispirited little fox that he has found Ferdy. "Look, Rollo's uncle has gone up to be with him," he says. "And see, here's that crow that led me to him. It's jolly lucky that I fed the bird and that it became so friendly or I might never have spotted your brother up there." Very soon Rollo arrives with a coil of strong rope that he wants to heave into the tree. At the sight of it the crow becomes curiously excited, squawking and flapping its wings right in Rollo's face.

Rollo is mystified. "I wish that bird would get out of my way," he says. "I want to toss this rope up to my uncle." Then Rupert starts forward. "That crow's cleverer than you think," he cries. "It has already helped me no end, and I believe it knows what you want. There are so many branches you couldn't throw the rope far. Let's see if the bird will do it for you." Taking the coil he offers one end to the crow. The bird immediately seizes it and flies up towards Ferdy.

RUPERT GIVES FERDY A RIDE

At last the man calls to the chums,
"Steady him down, now! Here he comes!"

Then he makes Ferdy stamp around,
To prove that he is safe and sound.

"We'll pull your brother for a while,"
The chums tell Freddy, with a smile.

Then they must go their separate ways,
"All's well that ends well," Rupert says.

While they wait anxiously the four friends can all hear noises far above them where the man is working, and at last comes his call, "Watch for it now! And steady him down!" Something appears swinging gently towards them and missing all the boughs of the tree. It is the sledge, with poor Ferdy tied to it, being eased down by the strong rope. When it is on the ground the man drops lightly beside it, helps Rupert to untie the cords, and then makes Ferdy stamp about in the snow to prove he is still unhurt. The chums help to make Ferdy feel warm again, and as he still seems rather dazed he is put on the sledge to be pulled back to their starting point by Rupert and Algy, while the clever crow, which seems as interested as ever, comes and perches on the snowman. Then Rollo and his uncle say that they will see the two foxes back to their home, and leave Algy and Rupert feeling very relieved that the accident was no worse and has ended happily.

RUPERT LIKES THE SNOW BEAR

*"Oh Mummy, I've so much to tell!
The crow comes into it, as well!"*

*Next day they hear a knock, rat-tat!
"Hello," frowns Rupert, "who is that?"*

*"Good morning!" beam the little friends,
"We've done our best to make amends!"*

*"We're sorry for our trick, and so
We've built a Rupert, all of snow."*

At last the two pals separate and as Rupert trots homeward he meets Mrs Bear near the cottage. "Sorry I'm late, Mummy," he calls. "We've had such an adventure and look, here's that bird that we fed still keeping near me. If it hadn't been for him we could never have . . . but come indoors. I'll tell you the whole story." Next morning soon after breakfast there comes a tapping at the door and voices are heard. "That sounds like the foxes again!" murmurs Rupert. "What can they want this time?" The foxes seem none the worse for the mishap. "We've something to show you," smiles Freddy. On the way to a hedge his brother Ferdy starts explaining. "It served me right to have that accident yesterday," he says. "We started out meaning to smash your snowman, so now we've made a special one all for you." Rupert gazes with delight at what they've done. "I say, you are clever!" he laughs. "It's just like *me!* It isn't a snowman. It's a snow Rupert!"

Bestall